KAJO

An Australian Adventure Romance

KAREN POWER

Published by Karen Power

Copyright @2021. The moral right of Karen Power to be identified as the Author of the work has been asserted by her in accordance with the Copyright, Designs and Patents Act 1988. All rights reserved. No part of this book may be used or reproduced by any means, graphic, electronic, or mechanical, including photocopying, recording, taping or by any information storage retrieval system without the written permission of the publisher except in the case of brief quotations embodied in critical articles and reviews.

This novel is entirely a work of fiction. The names, characters and incidents portrayed are the work of the author's imagination. Any resemblances to actual persons, living or dead, events or localities are entirely coincidental.

ISBN: 978-1-7635753-2-5 (paperback)
ISBN 978-1-7635753-3-2 (e-book)
ISBN: 978-1-7635753-5-6 (audiobook)

Book cover artist: www.selfpubbookcovers.com/JohnBellArt

A catalogue record for this book is available from the National Library of Australia

DEDICATION

To my dear Mother, who continually prays for me, and my friends, I thank you for your support to help me pursue my creative endeavors. Much love.

Karen Power xoxo

One

Year set 1985

Kaitlin, a pretty young woman, dressed in her pale blue pinstripe uniform, sits tensely as she drives her little car rapidly through the Adelaide City streets. She was running late for work and sighed, muttering to herself that that's all she needed, another red light and more messy road works to slow her down. Kaitlin would have to drive faster to get to work on time this morning. Going through the city in the early morning traffic was a huge unexpected challenge today, and she never liked speeding. That said, being late was the pits, and even worse for her, would be to arrive halfway through the Nursing handover. Her hair wasn't done correctly and escaped loose long dark red curls hung precariously. Aware more than likely, the Matron would reprimand her for her out-of-character shabby dress code today. Although the staunch Matron would have every reason to do so, personal appearance was of utmost importance in her expectation in the Nursing Fraternity. The Matron was, after all, old school, strict, and very regimented. If Kaitlin hadn't had such a late night, or should we say, such an early morning at the party, arriving home at 3.00 am, she would never have slept in, but no point in crying over spilled milk now it was way too late to complain about that.

Pulling into the doctor's car park, she parked her car. Deciding that would do for the moment, later she would come and move the vehicle once she was more organized early on in her shift. On checking her fob watch, realizing there were only three minutes to go, she ran into the Hospital Foyer, flying up the stairs arriving at the Nurses' Station, and quickly throwing her bag in the corner. Cordially greeting everybody, great thought Kaitlin, she made it just on time, and she realized she was working with Jo. Jo was a stunning, thin blond with absolutely startling blue eyes that were so true to her Scorpio character.

The team of nurses sat at the Nurses' Station behind the glass windows looking out onto the ward, while taking in the report and diagnosis of the patients being given by the gloomy night nurse. Kaitlin sat adjusting her starched uniform collar and adjusted her nurse's cap, then silently listened to all the goss regards what the night nurse had endured on the night shift. "There has to be a better job than this," Jo whispered to Kaitlin, who subtly nodded her head to agree. The way Kaitlin felt anything would be better than facing a full bedpan first thing this morning. The night nurse finished the handover and left the ward. Jo and Kaitlin commenced their early morning round, greeted all their patients for the day, and introduced themselves to all. Walking into one bay of four patients, drawing the curtains, saying so cheerfully,

"Good morning all, how are you?" The voice of gloom emerged from the bed, "I feel ill, turn out the lights go away, leave me alone." Jo, always having an answer, replied, "Sure would you like anything else to go with that order," both nurses quietly shaking their heads vacated the ward. The following two bays were similar. For sure, as Jo and Kaitlin agreed, many sick patients require and deserve such a great deal of compassion. Still, at times the two were undoubtedly challenged by some people acting like hypochondriacs for attention-seeking purposes, and they both wondered what had happened to those people in their lives to be that way.

Moving forward into the workload, the two organized all the patients to be showered, shaved, cleaned, scrubbed, powdered, pampered, and obligingly attended to almost their every whim. Hallelujah, it was their tea break. On the Senior Nurse in charge's instructions, they both ventured downstairs to the tea room for a quick break. They were sprawling into chairs to put their feet up to relax with an excellent hurried cup of coffee. Jo remarked about the morning's undertakings. "Now, how many happy patients have we struck this morning?" as she shook her head. "Not many," Kaitlin replied. "That's right," Jo said. "It's the same thing every morning. You psyche yourself up every morning to arrive at work happy. The first thing you do is walk into a patient's room, say, hello, how are you? They say, crap, and you get the same thing for the next five rooms. Who wants to work in this negative environment? I want to do something new. I want to get out of here."

Kaitlin's feelings were similar about it being a hostile environment. Although reflecting on Jo's words, Kaitlin thought that work is what you make it. There were many times when she received so much love and kindness from strangers who were so emotionally raw from their situations or palliative care patients dying. She responded to Jo in an attempt to encourage her. "For your work to work for you, you must put interest into it for it to be interested in you." Jo looked at Kaitlin with pursed lips pulling one of her theatrical faces, then agreed with Kaitlin by a slow lento nod. On many occasions, Kaitlin had an excellent rapport with her patients. She was immensely evolved and very spiritual at heart. Kaitlin's dream was to travel the world and write about it. The first place she wanted to go was Machu Picchu and trek through the Incas. She constantly had visions of doing that trek. One day this would eventuate, but in the meantime, the mortgage had to be paid, and everyday living attended to, and she knew only too well if you want to be successful, you have to do the work.

Jo dreamed of being a famous actress, but it wasn't going to fall into her lap like she envisaged and wished. She had to spend a lot of money attending classes, putting in many long hours working on her physical appearance, speech classes, singing classes, and whatever else necessary to perfect herself and her voice. Having to face reality seemed dreary to her unless she could come up with some way of making a quick buck. They both had resigned themselves to the fact that they might as well enjoy work for the time being while still working toward making their dreams come true. Kaitlin had faith that there had to be some shortcut to fortune. She didn't want millions, just enough to be comfortably happy and pursue her dream. The idea of becoming a self-made millionaire seemed to her far more appealing than just striking a big prize in the lottery.

That night Kaitlin visited her old friend Wally. He was a good friend and had been for many, many years. His wife had recently passed away from lung cancer, and he presently needed a lot of cheery company and someone to discuss his grieving emotions openly. In the conversation throughout the night, Kaitlin explained that she wanted to devise an idea that would produce a lot of money. Enabling her to quit nursing as the nursing work was starting to take its toll on her. Kaitlin knew he'd understand because he was so much into inspiring young people to achieve their goals and become successful. Wally was always helping others, and he was so clever with selling any ideas, the making of oneself, and understanding what it took to become a dynamic, successful person. He had all the tapes, books, and literature one could ever read on the topic, but alas, he had nothing that was a straightforward concept to develop nor any new ideas that would suit her needs to start working on. His only words of wisdom and philosophy to her were simple."Find a need and fill it," then, basically, if you have an idea to build on and create, the millions will flow. After they had drunk tea, he helped her list ideas and avenues that maybe she could explore. Some thought would come if she kept at it. It was something to think and ponder over in the next few weeks.

Jo was having a party on that Saturday night. Kaitlin arrived in her usual hippy attire, looking very fine and sexy in a Stevie N hippy kinda style. Fred, Jo's boyfriend, greeted her at the door with a quick peck on the cheek and a big friendly smile. Barney, Fred's beloved Boxer dog, was in tow, who smooched into Kaitlin's leg as she reciprocated by giving him a loving pat. Fred regarded Barney's behavior toward Kaitlin with warm endearment. Fred had such piercing eyes, very short dark hair. He almost looked like an educated college boy type, rather stocky but with a very fit-looking body. Jo and Fred complimented one another. A very athletic-looking couple. Jo had always been so supportive to Fred, especially over the last few months as Fred was still grieving over the sudden death of his father, Jimmy. Jimmy, was a hard-working, good family man with a touch of larrikin Irish gaiety. Jimmy had a stroke while out working on the farm. Fred and his father were great mates and ever so close. Fred had spent most of his life working with his father up on the family farm in the Riverland. Then a couple of years back, Fred had been offered a job in the construction industry by one of his father's oldest friends, Giuseppe. It seemed like a good opportunity at the time, so Fred moved to the city of Adelaide, where he met Jo and fell madly in love when they met at the Hospital. At the time, he had sustained a minor injury working on the construction site and came in to get the wound attended to. Jo was working in the Emergency Department at the time, and that was it. Instant fireworks!! Jo and Fred had a magnificent relationship, and it restored one's faith that there is fairy-tale romance left in the world. Kaitlin lived in the hope that she too would be a magnet for her soul mate and one day find true romance once again. But who knows, after the sudden death of her boyfriend Dave in a motorbike accident whom she still pined for, she had not been bothered looking for another boyfriend for a very long time. It was still raw and excruciating even though much time had passed. She was open to a loving relationship, although she knew when you're searching for it, it never happens, so maybe at this time, it still wasn't the time yet to be looking.

While the music blared at the party and people outside were dancing to the beat and a couple up in the corner outside hoping that no one would notice them discreetly smoking pot. Jo, Fred, and Kaitlin were inside and sat around the kitchen table drinking dandelion coffee. At the table, deep in a serious conversation, Fred explained to Kaitlin that he had suddenly lost his job at Giuseppe's Construction Company. The Family-owned Company had suddenly gone bust, which seemed to be under mysterious circumstances strangely. Fred said his father, Jimmy, would be so disappointed, and he was left feeling betrayed by the whole ordeal. Fred continued stating that he had been wrongly accused of some pretty wild accusations that he knew nothing about. Given his father's death several months ago, and this sudden dismissal from work was such a big blow to him as a person, Jo and Fred had decided they would leave Adelaide and move up to the farm on the Riverland. It seemed like a good idea for both of them, given that was where other members of his family lived. Fred had inherited part of his father's massive property, including one of the old blue-stone farmhouses. If they moved, Fred would at least have employment, and also, it would be beneficial for Jo, who could quickly obtain a nursing position in the local Hospital. There was plenty of work on the family farm and also fruit picking on many nearby properties. Kaitlin was happy for them, however, a tear swelled in her eye as she felt gutted and sad to think Jo would no longer be at her work place at the Hospital. However, she understood that's just one of the facts of life. No one ever knows what's in store next or where one could be working or living. As we never know what's going to come up in our life's journey.

A couple of weeks later, after they fully renovated their old Victorian House, it was snatched up by a real estate mogul, being an excellent time to sell, plus the location of Semaphore was fast becoming a popular yuppie beach suburb. Kaitlin helped Jo and Fred move up to their big old bluestone farmhouse nestled in the grapevines of Cobdogla, a sleeping town near Berri in the Riverland. It was best known for its incredible fruit supplies, grapes, wine producers, and scenic landscape views. There were rickety old windmills, miles, and miles of rows of healthy green luscious grapevines, old antique and second-hand mart stores, and the town's continually fluctuating seasonal population. That was mainly due to grape-picking season, which would be very soon. That's what Fred and Jo's intentions were, to pick as many grapes as possible, working outdoors for a change, seeking some good fresh country air while saving lots of money, and living a healthy, sustainable lifestyle. They wanted Kaitlin to stay up in the country with them as they felt she was like family. It was a great idea. Kaitlin really would have to sit down and seriously think about how that would work for her and if she would ultimately be happy to make such a big move as she was not a person that liked a lot of change. It would require serious consideration. After all, it did seem quite an appealing proposition, although Kaitlin had her house to think about and her garden to consider. She had spent a lot of time working in her garden, and all her herbs and veggies would die if she wasn't there to attend to them. Kaitlin returned home to her humble little abode in suburbia and missed both Jo and Fred terribly for days. They were basically like a brother and sister that she never had. She was an only child and always looked to make families where she went.

Jo came for a very brief visit to Adelaide three weeks later and stayed with Kaitlin. She had to attend to some urgent business to tie up her position at the Hospital and also go to a particular bookshop on the city's outskirts to buy a specific book for one of the teachers at the local school in Cobdogla, whom she had befriended. Being such an outgoing, lovable character, Jo hadn't taken long to get to know the local people and get accepted into the small farming community. The two headed off on their mission to the old Book Shop. Indeed, it was a strange premise, having a strong, alluring magical presence about it. The background music sounded like something out of the medieval era mixed with angelic tones. The music clicked and clanked and created a mystical atmosphere, which Kaitlin felt was relaxing on the senses. The shop contained books that seemed as old as the shop itself. It was owned by an old Wicca Woman. It was full of herbs, potions, massage oils, and incense. The outside walls of the shop were painted with bright multi-colored flowers and magical, beautiful designs. Jo and Kaitlin were in awe. They were amazed to think that a shop like this existed in Adelaide and their era. Both explored the shop with utter child-like fascination. "Wow," said Kaitlin as she picked up an ancient Grimoire Book. The two ran a muck in the shop.

Jo excited, reciting from some of the book's old incantations, decrees, and spells from those of the Dark Ages. They laughed as Kaitlin repeated one spell that would supposedly conjure up and present to her while in the realms of deep sleep, her future betrothed. They gabbled on in playfulness, imagining themselves as two white witches until they were suddenly made aware of an older Wicca Woman sitting out of sight, behind the counter who now stood to make her strong, stern presence known. She gravely forewarned them that such derisive sceptical dabbling and sarcasm would only bring them ill tidings and ruefulness. Instantly refraining from such undisciplined behavior, they looked at each other in silent reverie. Jo quickly bought the book sought for her friend. Kaitlin, for merriment and to continue on with attaining her goal of coming up with an idea, opting for a gorgeous book on love potions and spells. Unfeigned admiring, the book cover artwork, and its artistic interior. It was brilliantly beautiful, with little hearts and bows hand-painted on most of the gold leaf pages, and from that day on, it would remain one of Kaitlin's most treasured possessions.

They decided to take time out for a coffee at Sirens Bohemian Coffee House. While sipping their fine brew, they enthusiastically foraged through the books, discovering some of the magical old love spells. They laughed and joked while sitting on the coffee house balcony, occasionally watching below the windsurfers on the beach and being lucky enough to have the whole balcony of the coffee house to themselves. They were sitting together so peacefully content. It was such a comely day. The sun's rays perforated the cirrus clouds, causing the sea to sparkle and glisten like diamonds as a couple of dolphins frolicked jubilantly in the rolling waves in the ocean below. "Just imagine if these potions did work, they would be worth a fortune," stated Kaitlin. Jo agreed wholeheartedly,

"Yeah, all the little college girl yuppies would be buying the potion and using it to find their dream man, who would fall in love with them and treat them like a princess, guested Kaitlin. "Or perhaps he would be bewitched and then robbed of all his credit cards," cynically continued Jo with frivolity. Kaitlin suddenly stopped mid-air having a mammoth epiphany. "What a diabolic thought," with a great rush of Adrenalin. "That's it, that's it, that's the idea, just the concept we need to create," quipped Kaitlin euphorically. Their eyes sparkled at the discovery of the magical idea. Kaitlin had found the answer, feeling deep-seated intuitive confidence that the sorceress's love potion idea would be very successful. They read through the Grimoire book, hurriedly trying to find the page with all the ingredients for a spectacular spellbinding aphrodisiac love potion, but on the last page of the interior of the book, it stated, "Refer to Book 2," which they didn't have, nor knew where it existed. They were racing off on the hunt for the second edition of the book, and in such a hurry to leave Siren Bohemian Coffee House, almost having an accident and tearing away the tablecloth with them. Kaitlin, amidst making her mad dash, was caught up in the moment, saying to Jo, "You know what it's like when you get an idea and you can't get where you want to go quick enough because of being overwrought with the passion of it all.

Kaitlin taking off so fast in her car, it seemed like they both had joined up with the Klardy Race Team and were on their last fast-paced winning lap. They shot back into immediate reality while in the throes of being pulled over by the Radar, which was a bit of a hassle for the two time-wise. The young Police Officer was only doing his job and gave the very embarrassed Kaitlin a very severe warning. They were in a hurry to get back to the Wicca Woman's Shop before it closed, only just making it before closing time. The old Wicca Woman looked on with grave discontent as they entered her magical shop once again. When Kaitlin asked for her help, she was indeed reluctant to aid their quest. When the money exchanged hands, she stared Kaitlin straight in the eye, saying, "You don't need this book. You have the power within you. Deep in your essence, it emanates from within your soul." It was as though someone walked over Kaitlin's grave on her receiving such a remark, unsure whether it was flattery, a curse, or an outright put-down. Triumphant, they left the quaint old book shop in a hurry, Jo having to catch a bus back to her little country hick town.

Two weeks passed. Kaitlin had experimented tirelessly with creating the magical love potion and eventually decided to put the magical bottled love potion in a small bag with potpourri and attaching a small parchment paper written with a spell on it to add a little touch of magical old-world charm. They would have a design on the little bag, which would feature Jo and Kaitlin, dressed as witches in old century lace clothing looking mystical and witchy. The idea was similar to that of a female rock artist in the present, who had split from her famous Band recently then releasing her Solo Music Album, "Rock A." Kaitlin, at the time, was impatient and unable to find anything else she liked as a feature photo for the brand. Feeling it was still a slightly original idea that now seemed appropriate and complimentary for the finished product. They had to take sepia tones to make a print, and

Wally was just the one to help them out here, as he was an avid old photographic fanatic.

Kaitlin phoned Wally and let him know about the idea and what she had been creating. He thought it was great and was all for helping out to help her complete the concept. Having then to organize somehow a big fake picture frame, then paint flowers all around the border of the prop. Jo and Kaitlin had to come up with a name for the Love Potion, humming and harring, conjuring up ideas and thoughts over the landline constantly, trying to use their words somehow in the mix. After several phone conversations, they finally came up with "KAJO," which seemed rather appropriate by using the first two letters of their first names. Wally and Kaitlin spent many hours painting the feature frame prop for the upcoming photo shoot. Kaitlin went out shopping for old-world lace and materials that could be used to create the picture frame illusion. Wally and Kaitlin had many long, arduous nights working tediously and enthusiastically putting the ideas and artwork together, and they had many hilarious moments. The final result was truly magnificent and so beautiful.

The day for the photo shoot had arrived, and Wally and Kaitlin had driven to Cobdogla in one of Wally's big removal vans loaded with all the creative artworks. Amidst all the excitement, they all settled into the work. Seated in the picture frame was Kaitlin looking a picture of old-worldly loveliness, with her arm extended outward and forearm bent upward with what looked like a real dove but was a fake, bought from the local florist shop. Jo stood next to a small table, with a beautiful crochet lace cloth spread over it and a crystal ball in the center of the table. She was standing in an old-worldly silk gown, holding a sparkler, which gave one the impression of a magic wand. When Wally developed the photos, they were all so exquisite and mystical looking. He also took individual shots of both of them just in case they needed a little extra and also for their keepsakes.

The next job was to duplicate the photos onto a screen print. Then came the task of making small pouches out of calico, cutting them out, and sewing them up. That was probably the most tedious chore of the entire project, however, no one else was around to do that job. It seemed that now as they had made progress with the task, Kaitlin felt it was time to decide what avenue she would take regarding her employment situation. It had been such an exciting experience organizing this new venture. It was going to be incredibly difficult returning to work at the Hospital. Kaitlin wasn't looking forward to the feeling of being creatively stifled. Just in case, to hedge her bets. Before leaving Cobdogla as Kaitlin and Wally drove out of the small country town. Wally pulled up on the side of the road when Kaitlin saw a large advert posted on the gum tree that read, "wanted fruit pickers inquire within" there was also a phone number etched at the bottom of the sign. Just a little further down the road, she could see a phone box. Wally drove ahead after Kaitlin took down the phone number and then hopped in the phone box and rang the farmer and had a very positive conversation regarding work. Wally was pleased she had organized a temporary job grape picking that could possibly last for eight weeks or more, should she decide to throw caution to the wind, knowing deep down how impulsive one could be when on a quest. Although typically not Kaitlin's style to be that impulsive, at least she had created options. As they drove along the wondrous river-land landscape heading home, Wally assured Kaitlin, once again by his wise words, "When you have options, you have far more control."

If she did decide to move up here to Cobdogla, this would give her a chance to complete the creative project with Jo and still also earn some cash at the same time. Still needing to think more about the move, she recalled, as the old saying goes, when in doubt, don't. In the meantime, Kaitlin had decided to investigate and research their newfound magical love potion product, especially exploring all the herbs and oils required to construct this aphrodisiac magical love potion. Becoming very absorbed in white witchery was a fun thing initially and began to impact them. Their whole lives started to change due to this metaphysical change. Things started happening that was so noticeable. Since the time they'd ventured into the Gypsy shop, Kaitlin had now dyed her hair to a burgundy color. It was long and all wring-lets, and in recent photographs, she even looked a little bit mystical and witchy. Maybe it was just the dark eyes. Who knows? Fred had started dreaming about his dad, Jimmy, and even though he saw the ghost of Jimmy standing outside on the front verandah in the stillness one night. It scared Fred at first, but then Fred was happy to know that Jimmy was around and Fred could still talk to him in spirit. It seemed to help Fred to deal with the pain of such a great loss. Fred felt then that Jimmy's death didn't then feel so final and leave such an empty sad void. Jo began singing far more often and mimicking movie dialogue from the famous old movie starlets in practice for her own future dream.

Wally and Kaitlin arrived back in the city of Adelaide,

very enthused and invigorated by the whole weekend's inventive experience. He dropped Kaitlin back at her home late in the afternoon. She cheerily bid him farewell and then unloaded everything and hurriedly placed everything in its place, as she was such a tidy freak. Kaitlin then collapsed on her comfy couch as her mind was unrestrained with creative thought. She then began to fall asleep. Then about two hours later, suddenly she woke again, refreshed, full of energy and innovative ideas. That night for hours, she toiled away in the kitchen, experimenting with all the oils she had bought to improve her magical love potion perfume base to make it even better and smell far more intoxicating and divine.

Time had passed, Kaitlin sat comfortably on the bar chair, leaning on the sterile breakfast bench. New-Age Music was playing in the background. The Nag Char Incense burns, the gentle haze circulating throughout the kitchen, she read the two opened magic books, Her fingers follow the lines of the sentence, "I call to the Wicca Woman when the Moon is full at 7.00 pm collect'. Kaitlin stops amidst the sentence, checks her antique cuckoo clock. It's 5 minutes to 7.00 pm. Spontaneously she opens the thin Venetian blind pulling the cord to completely expose the clear glass of the large window. The rays of the beautiful full moon shine through, Kaitlin breathed a sigh of relief. She stared out at the clear night sky outside. As the stars twinkled in the sky and the moonbeams of light danced into her kitchen. Her black cat slinked graciously up into the windowsill, giving Kaitlin a loving look. She gently reached over and patted the cat's head. She dimmed the leading light in the kitchen. She sits focus-sing again, lighting five different colored candles, placing them in a large semi-circle on the bench. She opens the bottles of oils, placing them inside the semi-circle. Kaitlin checks the book for directions, pausing for a brief moment moving the books to the left inside the semi-circle. She puts the large glass bowl in the bench center, adding a teaspoon of blue allergy-free food dye. ½ a glass of distilled water, ¼ bottle of lavender, rose geranium, bergamot, rosemary, ylang ylang, sweet orange, grapefruit, lemon, and a snippet of sandalwood, then she stirs the mixture. She rechecks the book for direction. Placing in the bottom of the bowl a large amethyst and rose quartz crystal. Outstretching her arms up above her head, she looks toward the moon. Kaitlin speaks out aloud, "Fairies, Paralda, Leprechauns, and Zephyrs of the air. Your fun and love I really do now seek to share, Salamanders led by the Djin. The candles flames I invite you to come and play in. Put for me your magic of love in this magical love potion. So that it will attract to any a wearer, great love and complete unequivocal sincere devotion. I call to the metaphysical world to hear my request, this substance I place under the moonbeams for you to add magical energy to give this magical love potion its aphrodisiac zest."

Kaitlin circles her long crystal wand in the air three times. She circles the rod over the top of the bowl. She blows to the right. She blows to the left. She rings the crystal bell in the air to the right, then to the left. She rechecks her book. She stands to continue on with the ritual placing the bowl of love potion carefully on the windowsill. The moons' rays beam directly down into the magical substance. She stands back, she holds her hands in the air above the potion, her angelic face bathes in the dancing moonlight rays. The small black feline sits on the sink, smooching right up next to her. Kaitlin gently caresses her cat. She stares intensely outside the window. A miniature apparition of Venus walks down the moonbeam, walks through the glass of the windowpane, and hovers like a beautiful little butterfly over the magical love potion substance in the clear glass bowl. The pretty little spirit blows a kiss of fairy-like dust into the magic potion. Venus turns into a mired of starry colors circling over the bowl several times before diving into the magical elixir. Eros appears in miniature form and shoots gold arrows into the substance. The light apparition of the Wicca Woman's face appears floating over the potion. The cat leans over and flicks at the Wicca Woman's face with her paw. She meow's, instantly. Kaitlin scolds the cat, who now struggles to get out of Kaitlin's grasp. The tiny Eros apparition drops swiftly into the love potion, swimming and swirling around, disappearing into the magical love potion. Kaitlin puts the cat down on the floor, chiding her, "Oh, look what you've done! You scared them away. I hope you haven't messed up my spell, Slinky. The cat looks back at her and frowns, then goes back over to the couch, lazing on the couch and sulks from a distance.

Kaitlin glares back at the cat, then back to the love potion, trying to re-create the same mood. She rechecks the Spell book, she looks at her scribbled note of ingredients, she waits for a moment, nothing happens. Kaitlin breathes an exasperated sigh. She turns all the lights back on. She madly hunts through medieval magazines, gazing at various pictures. The CD ends. Moving to the cabinet in the living room, she selects a different CD pulling the CD cover out from the shelf. She stares at it, reflecting for a moment.

Kaitlin rips the paper cover out from the CD holder. She walks back into the kitchen, spreading the paper cover across the picture in the magazine, which lay open on the bench. Standing around to compare them. She checks the magical love potion on the windowsill. Kaitlin sits down again on the bar chair. She picks up the landline and dials a phone number.

Two

Kaitlin returning home from the Hospital, was so glad to close the front door behind her. It had been a really long hard day, and Kaitlin was totally exhausted from the grind of it all. Overloaded with complaints from various patients and the feeling of disillusionment hanging heavy over her heart, Kaitlin entered the lounge room and, flopping onto the large comfortable sofa, picked up one of her new books titled "Crystals and their healing life." Interestingly, although somewhat foreign to her, in her great thirst for further evolved knowledge on the mystic, it seemed appropriate content to read right now. The book explained how to use the Quartz Crystal as a tool to focus on activating one's creative powers within. Following the directions in the book. She placed the crystal, which she had bought from the Wicca Woman's Shop, above her head on the couch while lying flat on her back, and she tried to relax. Kaitlin was so tired now she really didn't know if she could be bothered with this experiment right now. She began to drift into a deep, deep sleep. Her mind was hazy. Her spirit pelted back to the Hospital with the Nurses and Doctors standing around chanting, "Take the key, take the key." A pleasant stranger held the key in his hand. He reached out to her, offering the key to her. In the dream, she started screaming, "No, no, let me out."

Kaitlin grabbed the key, turning away to run to try and get out. It seemed like her body was running in prolonged motion and wasn't getting anywhere fast. Suddenly behind her, there was a giant rubber dark grey door. In her dream distorted vision, it extended upward and stretched for miles. She looked at it for a moment, then struck the door. It wobbled, and the sound was loud and echoed for a long time through her mind. She became panic-stricken as she couldn't pass through the door. Her heart began racing. Pulling frantically at the door handle, she found the door moved animated out of shape. Sadly it still remained tightly shut. The loud nurses' chants faded into the background. When she turned around, the nurses melted into a pile of snow, which dissolved down into a drain hole that appeared on the floor where she stood. Then upshot a white projector screen before her eyes. The projector came up from the drain hole. The film on the big white screen started rolling.

There on the screen, appearing before her, was an old nurse, very grey-headed and wrinkled. She stood there chatting to a patient who was lying in bed with his broken leg elevated. The old woman in her pinstriped uniform was offering him a bedpan. The old woman looked very familiar, but Kaitlin wasn't sure who she was. Moving curiously closer to the screen. This old woman was so familiar Kaitlin wasn't sure where she knew her from. Now Kaitlin moved next to the screen, reaching out to touch it, and as she did so, the old women suddenly became aware of Kaitlin's presence. Kaitlin, too could now clearly see the old woman. The old woman stared sternly back. Her wrinkled face held a look of great disdain. The old woman's face grew bigger, shocking Kaitlin, who suddenly realized she was actually looking at a much older version of herself.

Kaitlin screamed a shrilling, blood-curdling scream as the old woman's whole face grew until it took over the entire length of the projector screen. Astonied, Kaitlin fell backward into the door, her body frozen by panic-stricken fear. Her hands came up to hide her face from the old woman and then aware the key was still in her grasp. Turning instantly to face the door, she stuck the key into the keyhole. It fitted. She twisted it in the lock, the door flew open. Jumping away from the room, looking back, she saw the old woman's gigantic hand reaching out to grab her. She slammed the door closed to lock out the ogre. Safe now behind the doors. Kaitlin could breathe easily. Aware she now stood in a type of historical museum with paintings, sculptures, and many different features, also very modern-day technology, with futuristic computers and specialized machines that one couldn't even put a name to, nor had one ever seen before.

Next, while wandering through this picturesque maze, she stopped before large five-foot glass cylinders. On top of them were perfume bottles luxuriantly displayed of the top ten most Exclusive Perfumes in the World. In the most enormous cylinder, standing exquisitely presented under beautiful lighting, was a bottle of "KAJO," Kaitlin's heart leaped.

Momentarily startled, someone gently tapped her on the shoulder. Turning to look, she discovered it was a warm dashing young gentleman dressed with sophistication in a tuxedo.

He smiled sweetly and informed her he would escort her out. As she proceeded to walk, the enormous heavy gold theatrical curtains directly in front of them began to open. Looking down, she realized she was now dressed in a beautiful neon pink off-the-shoulder sparkling knee-length, body-hugging sexy dress, feeling fabulous.

Before her, an extraordinary marble-floored stage. The stage lights went on, and the applause went up. There were hundreds of people sitting in the audience in front, clapping and whistling. The gentleman escorted her to the right of the colossal imperial stage, where surprisingly Jo appeared. She stood dressed in an impressive royal blue gown similar to Kaitlin's and looking implausibly luminous with happiness.

Jay Martin greeted both and congratulated the two for winning the first prize Award. They were presented with the significant Gold Award. Both feeling as though they had just won a Global Golden Award, being ascent upon by flashing lights, TV News, and press cameramen. Both filled with a significant surge of excitement, Jo gave a short speech of thanks. Then it was Kaitlin's turn on the podium to speak and thank whomever. Unprepared and unable to think where to start with her address. As Kaitlin was opening her mouth to greet the audience, a loud telephone rang. The audience became a haze, and then an incredibly oversized telephone appeared before her. It rang and rang. It drowned out the dream. Her mind now only holding a blurry vision. Suddenly she was awake again. Shaking her head back into reality, talking to herself. "God, it was only a dream. My god, what a terrible dream and yet so prophetic. That's it". She was determined to quit work that day. Then second thought set in, deciding that maybe the best thing to do would be to take a few months' special leave. After all, what did she have to lose? There was no way she wanted to end up like the old grey nurse. That was undoubtedly one of the worst nightmares and an astronomic wake-up call to help Kaitlin move forward with Jo and the Magical Love Potion Project. Immediately she rang Wally and then was going to ring Jo, having decided to pack all her gear and head up to Cobdogla so the two of them could create the magical love potion and get it out to the world and see if it would sell. The two had nothing to lose. It would be an adventure indeed.

The phone rung again loudly. Answering the phone, Kaitlin heard Jo's voice come across the landline. Jo was becoming more psychic since delving into this white witchcraft. She seemed almost mentally in tune with Kaitlin. She said that she had been thinking about Kaitlin and felt there was something wrong. Kaitlin then explained her dream to Jo. It really was a great sensation knowing she had the choice to choose her own future. Jo was ecstatic when Kaitlin asked if she could stay with them for a little while and work up at Cobdogla and if they could start to work on creating the magical love potion "Kajo" together.

Kaitlin rang the Hospital to request special leave right away. Probably not one of the most responsible moves she'd ever made, but then again, there's nothing like spontaneity, even though it was way out of character for Kaitlin. The mere excitement of it adds spice to life. Packing all her clothes together so fast and throwing them in, she could hardly shut the suitcase.

Ally, a nursing friend of Kaitlin's, was more than willing to live in the house for a couple of months and happily pay some weekly rent. It was nice to make someone happy helping them out with accommodation and to know that her beautiful little house was in good hands. Before long, Kaitlin was driving off on her journey. Without an inkling of the future, but thrilled by the adrenaline rush of the exhilaration of it all. Her thoughts were racing the unfamiliar feeling that it was so right and in her mind no fear or doubt as to her present actions. Kaitlin's confidence soared, thinking to herself, as Mum would say, "Never argue with a hunch. Christopher Columbus followed a hunch, and for that fact, look how famous he was in the making of history based on his hunch."

So the only thing to fear was fear itself. Kaitlin's current situation was momentarily so strange. It was as if she were following some sort of lead, like something or someone had given her an order, and her being, following so promptly and quite happily with no doubting.

As she drove farther on to her destination as time passed, it became an incredibly overwhelming feeling. The miles passed quickly along with her thoughts, the Australian Riverland scenery amazing. The Murray River was beautifully still, unencumbered and scenic, giving one a vivid illustration of the Australian wildlife. The colorful bird life nestled in the gangling gum trees that had stood in the water, sturdy, solid, and tall for centuries.

Three pelicans flew low in single file against the picturesque warm blue sky. Almost skimming the water, then diving down to collect a feed of fish, which reminded Kaitlin, it was nearly tea-time. It would be good to end the journey and joyously greet old friends. Their warmth and sincerity was reassuring, much appreciated, and something to really look forward to.

Three

Arriving soon after dark at the farm, she quickly unpacked. With Jo and Kaitlin's mouths vigorously working overtime, desperate to get a word in, the conversations moved quickly with laughs, sighs, and slight touches of affection. It was like one of them had just returned from years abroad in the Sahara Desert. Jo and Kaitlin excitedly set up their life-size photographs and placed them in a sizeable old picture frame that had been restored, mounting them onto the entry hall wall. They decided to put the old roller top desk underneath against the wall. Then into the escritoire, they placed all the parchment papers, spell books and plans, and ingredients for the love potion.

While Kaitlin had been busy in the city, Jo had now been working at the local Hospital where she had befriended a very young woman, Emily, a 20-year-old pretty petite little blond, who temporarily had moved in with Jo and Fred. She was in the situation of being pregnant to one of the guys, who was one of the Anglo biker gang that lived about half a kilometer down the road, on an astronomic property. Emily was destitute, deeply depressed, and unable to decide what to do regards the baby. Emily knew she was so young and had no mothering experience as yet. Emily didn't think she could have an abortion because she loved her little one already and could feel it growing beautifully every day. She had morning sickness very severely, and Jo had offered Emily a temporary home and helped her as much as she could. Emily was overly quiet at times, but Jo, Fred, and Kaitlin made so much noise together it was hard for her to make herself heard. At times Emily became very depressed and forlorn. One could understand that it must have been traumatic for her in her present situation. Besides, she had come from an unusual background. Her parents had separated when she was a child. Her mother remarried a gentleman who didn't want the stepdaughter around. He was incredibly wealthy and sent Emily off to boarding school, which she hated. She then decided to rebel. Emily then became involved with drugs. It was, in actual fact, Emily's cry for help, but her mother refused to recognize it or reassure Emily in any way. After being expelled from one college after another. One of her young friends dragged her off to the drug and alcohol center for her to dry out and get her act together. She had extensive counseling and worked hard to kick her short-lived drug habit. During that time, she met her ex-boyfriend Brian, who now belonged to the Anglo biker Gang. Brian had initially moved to the area for the grape-picking season and then decided to join the Anglo biker gang. Since joining them, he became aggressive verbally to Emily and ended their relationship, hence unknown to anyone, she took refuge at Jo and Fred's farm.

Meanwhile, down the massive back shed situated a short distance from the main blue-stone farmhouse, Kaitlin, Jo and Fred, had fun with the majestic love potion creation. Although Kaitlin had already created a mighty potent love potion before arriving back at Fred's Farm. They s till had much merriment researching all the oils to see what other alternative potions they could create. Jo, Fred, and Kaitlin spent many nights experimenting with oils, essences, powdered herbs, and crushed flowers, t rying t o c ome u p with another rare beautiful aphrodisiac perfume that would melt any man's heart and turn him blind with passion. Fred had even made a large witches' cauldron for them to stir up all the magical love potions. What joy they had. They s oon hit the jackpot and created a different love potion which Barney the Boxer dog didn't seem to like as much as Kaitlin's magical aphrodisiac heady love potion. Shortly after, they all reverted back to Kaitlin's original magical love potion she had initially created. The potion Kaitlin had made was almost accidentally created. They decided that w as the o ne. Th at was the actual birth of "KAJO," the magical love potion. They a ll decided this was what they were looking to create and would be proud of as a selling product and brand. They all a greed, t his was the absolute best potion. Lucky for them, Kaitlin's attention to detail had seen Kaitlin write all the ingredients down. Otherwise, one would never have been able to remember such a mixture. It was a hellishness of a concoction. Not quite eatable for Barney, the Boxer dog, though. But the smell was delicately divine oriental musky notes and highly sensual. For any man to smell it, he'd feel like he'd been knocked out into paradise. It was very heady. Poor old Barney, the Boxer dog, was besotted by its potent aromatic powers.

Jo got out the Piral White Champagne, handing the glasses

all-round. After days of long hours and experimenting, they'd done it. What exhilaration actually discovering and creating two beautiful new perfumes. Looking around, realizing the shed was a complete shambles. What an experience, what a feeling! It looked as though the shed hadn't been tidied for weeks, Kaitlin speaks out about their current surroundings, "you have to sacrifice a bit to gain a bit." Devouring the Champagne after two glasses, they become reasonably merry, as none of the three were great drinkers at all, and after all, this was a rare occasion. There was great cause for celebration, and besides, it wasn't as if one had the responsibility of driving home on the roads and endangering someone else's life. They drank their third celebratory glass and decided to put their glasses down, deciding everything in moderation and too much alcohol can be bad for your health anyway. Then the three, for fun, pledged an oath of secrecy. They wrote their names on parchment, sealed it with a short good luck spell which Jo, caught up in the magical moment suggested, and readout of her new spell book, and a drop of blood was added from each of their fingers for reassurance. Barney, the Boxer dog, happily hovered around them, sharing in the magical love potion energy. It would be sure to bring them some good luck as they were only sending out good positive vibes with the spell, so they thought. Kaitlin read aloud more incantations from the ancient Grimoire book for the love potion to become a powerful aphrodisiac. She also read aloud from the book to the other two, "That's the thing with white witchcraft. It's only for doing good. Once you start sending out negative vibes and curses to people, that's meddling into all the black witchcraft, and that's a big no-no because, in the long run, you only draw incredibly bad karma." Emily really hadn't been all that interested in their project so far, which was probably for the best. After all, they didn't want the new creation divulged to anybody even though she seemed harmless enough. Kaitlin and Jo were excited and proud that they'd actually put their dreams and ideas into reality and had now created the magical love potion "KAJO." The next minute, Kaitlin was ringing Wally to inform him of the brilliant magical love potion they had concocted. Now they also needed to know the next step towards marketing it, as he was definitely the man to speak to about that topic, for sure. The feeling of outstanding achievement was rife in the farm household. Wally was excited for Kaitlin and her friends and made a wise comment as she stood listening to his voice on the landline. "It just goes to show, if you dream, if you can believe in your dreams, you can make it happen. It's a matter of putting your thoughts into physical action and sticking to the goal. Because it can happen when it's meant to be, it's just a matter of time. If all your efforts don't work, at least you had the guts to make a go of it, you've gained strength, you've gained knowledge and experience, then if all else has failed, you can always try something else. As long as you keep going, you are bound to be successful at some point." Kaitlin really thought deeply about Wally's words of wisdom he was imparting, and in this case, she definitely had to agree.

Four

Emily's ex-boyfriend Brian, a tall thin, determined young man, impetuously arrived at the Hospital just as she finished her shift. He marched up to her wanting to discuss their situation and his feelings for her. Emily caught utterly of guard, was very reluctant to reciprocate, desperately trying to escape from him as she didn't want any scenes at the Hospital in her place of work, It was apparent that he was genuinely concerned for her welfare and had intense feelings for her. He was seeking peace of mind for himself. He wanted to know what was happening and where she was staying as he was concerned for his child's future. He explained that he wanted to be involved with, and be recognized as the father, and somehow be a part of the child's life. He didn't want his child to be an orphan like himself. Brian wanted the child to grow up with a mother and father who cared for it, even if they didn't live together.

Emily arrived home at the farmhouse for dinner, distressed and highly emotional. They all discussed the matter and decided to take Kaitlin's advice on how this would play out. Then guided by Kaitlin, Emily telephoned the boyfriend, advising him that he could visit her briefly in the hope that they could discuss their present predicament and work out a solution. He arrived about half an hour later at Fred's farmhouse. Surprised indeed by the protectiveness of Fred, Jo, and Kaitlin. And was made well aware of the impalpable boundaries in place regards this meeting and discussion.

Jo, Fred, and Kaitlin watched a video in the rustic old lounge room. Nestled comfortably on the old leather chesterfield set close to the warm large crackling open fire, discretely and quietly discussing the defunct couple's situation even though it really wasn't any of their business. They were relieved not to be in the same situation as the two people down in the kitchen. Fred going down the corridor ever so quietly in a fatherly fashion to ensure Emily was o.k. and reporting back to Jo and Kaitlin, who were snuggled up in the lounge room waiting for the update. At least they were acting like adults and actually sitting down to express their views, ideas, and feelings in a mature adult manner. That's how it should be, total honesty. None of those ridiculous little psychological games. Communication is the fundamental basis of a relationship and is required by both parties. The only way to resolve a problem is to talk it through and work out a favorable resolution, especially if you have a little one on the way. Fred sat back on the sofa, placing his muscle-bound arm around Jo in a loving Fashion. She smiled warmly, agreeing with his words.

Emily, deciding impulsively to try and make a go of the relationship again. Emily entered the lounge room, explained her plans to Fred, Jo, and Kaitlin, then went and swiftly packed. While she left the room to do so, the threesome made

Brian seem as comfortable as possible. Given the circumstances. Surprisingly enough for such a thin-looking young character, he was rather pleasant and was taken back and incredibly pleased that he had been made to feel accepted and at home in Fred's big old warm farmhouse. He almost didn't want to leave. Fred made his dominant overprotective point very clear, "It always pays to take people as you find them. sometimes when you take someone by personal appearance, you can significantly underestimate them, leading you to make a serious mistake." Brian agreed with Fred. The couple was seemingly content about their decision to try one more time to make the relationship work, and much love went with Emily that all would be well for her. She was sad but knew they would be there for her if she needed them again.

The couple eventually arrived back at the biker house late that night. At the biker property, a group of bikers sat around stoned, except for Rob, who was the leader of the biker gang, who didn't even smoke cigarettes. Rob was focused on the work in front of him, his facial features very defined with a rugged, handsome manliness. They were mixing up some concoction that would be used to fertilize the massive marijuana crops growing in all the greenhouses outside hidden amongst the cautiously planted tons of very high lush green tomato plants. The sprinkling system was high-tech for the day, and the product was almost ready for the street, with a price that would fetch well over a million dollars. Some members of the group went grape-picking while the others worked on the crop every day. There were definitely entirely clone-like in appearance. It was challenging to tell some of them apart.

There were about eight of them working on the cannabis crop project twenty four seven.

Finished for the day, the leader, Rob, sat in the lounge room, which was a far cry from homely looking, with worn-out old chairs and motorbike parts scattered about the large room. It was evident by the enormous mess that Emily had been away. The cleanliness within the residence had deteriorated immensely. Rob enquired to one of the guys as to Emily's return. Shortly after, Emily wandered into the kitchen. "So chic, how are you?" He smiled. He appeared a bit of a rough diamond with an unusual cultured speaking voice. He looks incredibly handsome, with soft brown eyes, olive skin, well-disguised under a long dark beard. His model-like body could match any one of the exclusive jean ads models on TV.

Unbeknown to his criminal assistants, his parents were affluent and owned one of the most well-known estates in Sydney. His mother was incredibly renowned as a celebrity socialite, her outings always photographed, her expensive taste noted, and many marriages to wealthy men always in the gossip columns.

Rob was the black sheep in his family and kept his background hidden from his present group surroundings. His family wanted him to achieve great success and planned out his life without consulting him on the subject. This had enraged him all his life. He rebelled, and, much to his mother's disgust, he had recently joined a biker group and adopted a rougher vocabulary and lifestyle in the process of initiation. Although he tried to hide and bury his past, Emily secretly knew from various newspaper clippings she had collected, who he may be, but was too scared to question him concerning her discovery. Her keen interest involved keeping tabs on the rich and famous. She was definitely an enthusiast of this topic. This was probably one of her only passions, and when she had spare money, she bought magazines or read the newspaper with intensity. She had secretly always aspired to be successful and hoped when she was older. That she would be, although she didn't know at what.

Explaining to Rob about her recent adventure, she expressed her deep feelings of appreciation toward Kaitlin, Jo, and Fred and innocently unintentionally revealed their secret money-making potent drug potion that's what she called it. Still, really she didn't know a lot about what it was. Rob was overly curious, and everyone else in the room became interested in listening in on their conversation. Rob immediately arrogantly decided they would steal the potent drug potion. After all, it sounded like a moneymaker even though he only half-listened to Emily's take on what it actually was. Emily knew only a tiny amount about the project, and she became distraught by the mere thought of the Bikers stealing the product from Kaitlin, Fred, and Jo, Emily's heart now panic-stricken. Brian, her boyfriend, rushed to her defense, questioning Rob's tactics and explaining what a great bunch of people they seemed and why not leave them alone. Brian made it clear that it may not even be a street drug that could be sold on the streets?

Rob disagreed and stood up ardently, stating he was the leader of this biker gang. If they didn't go along with his rules, they could pack their gear and leave and not even get a sniff of their soon-to-be payout from the upcoming drug deal sale. The biker group worked out a plan and interrogated the fearful Emily. She begrudgingly poured out information about the bikers' newfound prey so they could work out a way to steal this so-called potent drug potion. Rob, being so highly intelligent, devised a plan by which the finger would not point to them. Still, it would mean that he would have to case the property over the next week or so and investigate where Jo, Kaitlin, and Fred lived, recording details of the surrounding farmhouse and area.

Jo, Fred, and Kaitlin had packed up the last box of magical love potion perfume. They moved it all to the shed attached close to the blue-stone farmhouse, and the erotic aromatic smell had wafted right through the premises. The Boxer dog was so magically addicted to its imbuing perfume. The product was almost ready to be put on the market. The three of them now had to return to the city to explore Wally's avenues and ideas for promotional advertising, register the small business, and make inquiries about enlisting the patent on the magical love potion aphrodisiac product.

Jo and Kaitlin drove into the local township to the milk bar to pick up a few groceries. While there, they ran into Emily, who was unfortunately with one of the other members of the biker group. Jo casually mentioned that they were off to the city for a short trip, and if she needed anything to give them a call, they'd collect it for her while they were away in the city. Kaitlin felt a strange shivering chill run down her spine but not understanding why she felt unusual vibes emanating from Emily's friend. He wore the most scrupulous smirk on his face. Kaitlin felt, momentarily, unforgettable grief, but to no avail, could pinpoint or did she acknowledge her intuition and brushed it aside, thinking nothing more of it. Parting warmly from Emily, they returned on their journey home while Emily and her friend roared past on his extroverted hotted-up motorbike. It was, without doubt, a beautiful machine immaculately kept and honed brilliantly, leaving Jo and Kaitlin puttering along in Fred's reliable immaculate retro pale blue car. When arriving home with the goods, they set about making a tasteful vegetarian dish. The atmosphere in the old farmhouse was highly pleasurable and warm. The meal was the most decent they'd eaten in a week due to being so absorbed in such an experimental creation of the magical love potion project. The farmhouse was given a good spring clean. It really did need a clean. Jo and Kaitlin stopped cleaning the hallway and stood back momentarily to admire the beautiful mystical photographs that now hung on the wall and were so engaging, lit up by the candlelight of the hallway.

In the last few weeks, they had experienced a great abundance of blithe, which now seeped through the walls. From everything contained within, anybody who entered the farmhouse was almost devoured by vibrations of enchanted happiness. They checked on their last-minute packing, listing their priorities for the new business, ensuring that everything was organized for the forthcoming journey to market their product in the big city.

Five

Emily and her picaroon assailant, Carlos, a shady Spanish-looking character, returned to their abode house. Emily's emotions were now full of contempt toward some of the biker members plot to raid her dear newfound friends' farmhouse, where she had enjoyed many happy memories and joined in many laughable occasions in her short stay there. Carlos divulged to Rob the info that her friends were off to the city for a few days, which would allow the bikers to break in and steal the potent drug potion. Carlos had found out it was stored in the shed at the back part of the farmhouse property. On discovering the criminal plan, Emily, beside herself with anxiety, tried to warn her friends of the coming ordeal inconspicuously. Brian was dead against ripping the innocent three off of whatever they were producing. Brian also attempted to devise a plan to forewarn the threesome. Still, Emily's and Brian's attempts were futile, as they were unable to venture from the biker house through fear of getting caught by Rob, the leader. Brian's main concern was protecting Emily and their unborn child.

The power that Rob, the leader, possessed and yielded

was incredible. Even though he didn't contribute much in conversation with the other bikers, he remained distant and separated emotionally. He basically had their financial future in his hands. Therefore they were indebted to him until they received their cut of money from the upcoming drug crop. Therefore, no one stepped out of line, but the only power someone has over you is the power you give them. It was a difficult situation, as secretly Brian feared most of all for his safety, and he wanted enough money to leave the biker house as soon as possible and set him and Emily up in a comfortable, safe family environment. Although his ulterior intentions were possibly good, it was the actual deed carried out to achieve it that wasn't necessarily a good omen. As Brian and Emily knew, if you play with fire, you're bound to get burnt.

Emily eyed Rob, who sat there pondering, deep in thought, baring almost a look of slight vulnerability. She was aware that his heart was good underneath his rough facade. Rob ordered everybody into the lounge, where they all accumulated quickly at his demand. They sat with quiet anticipation, awaiting his verbal plan of action. He stated they must act promptly and with great precision to obtain this powerful drug potion. Nighttime seemed the most appropriate to strike. There would be no one about, meticulously ensuring there were no tracks or traces left in the surrounding vicinity, from either footprints or transporting vehicles, no fingerprints, no mistakes, not a shred of evidence, as to who committed the crime. That night Rob stole like a cat burglar into the stillness of the night to prey upon his innocent, unaware victims. Unfortunately, Fred had devised an excellent security system for the shed to protect the magical love potion. The job was not going to be easy, and specific tools would be required. Rob paced it all out in his mind, possessing the most remarkable criminal sense. However, some criminals who get away with certain crimes do have an outlandishly high level of genius, and they only commit crimes for the sheer thrill of the chase. Unfortunately, they just haven't learned to channel their intellectual energy into the right areas acceptable to the so-called norm in our society.

Carlos hot-wired the truck. It started up. The motor roared from its monstrous engine, Carlos happy they were in business with the truck's motor starting. Farmer Green, their neighbor on the farm next door to the biker group, was away on vacation. How convenient and no one would notice one of his trucks was missing off the property for a short span, as he basically lived the life of a hermit in seclusion. Farmer Green's truck was similar in appearance to all the others used in the local farming areas. That particular model was designed to dump all the grape produce into it before transporting it to all the local wineries. Most of the trucks that did the grape pickups were operated only at starlight hours, so they wouldn't even recognize farmer greens truck as being out of place. Carlos sped quickly in the stolen truck back to the biker property to pick up Rob and his small group of accomplices.

They quickly bailed into the truck, careful not to damage their own equipment. Silence remained among the small biker group as they clenched the railings for support as Carlos sped off recklessly. Rob thought instantly what a maniac driver Carlos was, secretly praying they would at least return home safe and sound that night. While vowing to himself that Carlos would never get the job as the driver again. In this frightful plight, clutching the railing for dear life, his head turned up toward the open canopy through which shone the light of the full moon. It was the eeriest feeling, almost as if, some ghostly being, were watching. The thought sent a slight unnerving shiver through his body. They drove slowly through the vines as unperturbed as possible. Carlos hit the brakes. Such a sudden jolt caused one of the crew, Rolf, who was a really big tall guy, to bang his skull on the iron wall by which he clung. The pain was immensely severe but totally suppressed because of his present situation requiring no noise.

A streak of dark fluid flowed down his face. He licked it and, with the taste of warm blood smearing his tongue intensely cursing Carlos under his breath, Determined to definitely sort him out on their return trip to the biker property. With no time to think, upon arrival at their destination, they jumped from the truck as swift and as gracious as greyhounds. Heading in the dark fleetly to unlock the large door to the old brick unused pickers hut at the rear end of Fred's farmhouse property. Aware that just inside the door was an expanding ladder that Rob, unbeknown to many, had placed there the previous night in anticipation of tonight's premeditated theft. They glided it out of the hut without a sceric of noise. Equipment in hand, they leaned the ladder against the shed wall and, in single file, speedily climbed to the top of the roof. The large clear moon provided much light for the visibility of their next move. Rob proceeded to cut a large hole in the roof of the big shed with a blow torch. To provide ample room for them to haul the boxes of the powerful drug potion out using a thick rope absailing pulley, without arousing a single sign of setting off Fred's well-put-together screeching security system, Rob admired the brilliance of Fred's security system. He secretly admired himself more and felt extolment for being able to break through the clever security system.

Once inside the large shed, they had to maintain a close vicinity to the center of the room. Otherwise, the sensors would alert the alarm, setting it off loudly and offensively like an air raid siren to other farmers on nearby properties. Rob checked his watch to ensure they were on schedule. The men needed to hurry. They were running out of time. Ensuring that everyone covered their positions, Rob quickly attached the ropes to the pulley system, which he had devised, hooking one on then slowly hoisting one box up to ensure it worked. Then the box was on its way up to the roof. It was then passed on to another chap, who passed it on to another guy, situated halfway down the ladder, who then passed it to one of the four chaps running the boxes over to be loaded in the truck. A primitive system of method of attack but necessary in this case. They were flat out, moving cautiously like cats on a hot tin roof to avoid getting caught by anyone.

Rob hoisted the last box up, and the signal was given to commence their next move. Now out of the large old shed, Rob ran along with a tiny pencil torch facing close to the ground, checking that the footprints left by his accessories were located only on the meagre dirt track. These would soon be dissolved of any visible evidence of their crime. Rob was now running. They were losing time. The crew packed themselves back in the truck, and so far, with no chance of their plot stuffing up, Rob jumped into the passenger seat of the truck. "Carlos, get out and set the timer." "What? Carlos looked at Rob confused. I'm the driver now," said Rob. "Do it!" stated Rob, practically pushing him out the door, then he moved across to the driver's seat. Carlos reluctantly ran into the grape pickers' shed. Carlos knew the system well. Rob and he had gone over it, if not a thousand times. He neared the machines and reset the timing mechanisms. This would then cause a power surge during the next few seconds, which would trip the overload switch, causing the automatic timer to reset at the wrong time. Then the sprinkling systems would be set off. Thus, a small flood of water would rush to the surrounding vicinity, washing away any footprints or tire prints left on the ground.

Carlos turned to dash. He pulled up with a sudden halt. His heart skipped a beat, and momentarily he lost his breath as his body froze dead in his tracks. Before him, staunch and mean, stood Barney, the Boxer dog. His eyes narrowed. His protective sinister growl revealing his sharp teeth. Carlos was petrified. He had a real phobia about dogs. Barney proceeded intensely to threaten Carlos slowly, one step at a time. Carlos began to perspire profusely, stealthily veering to the right toward the door in an attempt to get out. Barney went at Carlos instantly, his jaws and sharp teeth just missing Carlos.

Meanwhile, unaware Rob waiting in the truck, became impatient as he knew the sprinkling system was about to go off any second. Rob started to reverse the truck. Carlos quickly moved in a headstrong attempt to flee through the grape picker hut door. Barney's jaw clutched at his trousers. Carlos screamed, running like a wild banshee to the truck.

He punched Barney on the nose to get him away from his leg so Carlos was free to escape..

As the truck started to speed up in reverse, Carlos jumped up to the truck's step, holding on to the passenger's door. With one almighty leap, Barney pounced and sunk his teeth into Carlos's ankle. He locked his jaws and tore at the raw flesh. With his free leg, Carlos aggressively kicked Barney. The dog yelped from the shock and the pain and let go of Carlos's leg. Carlos, badly wounded, hastily bundled himself into the truck. Barney scurried, barking frantically and chasing in hot pursuit at the reversing speeding truck. Carlos, safely inside the cabin, now nurtured his severe painful bleeding open wound, excreting foul, angry Spanish slang words of abuse at the dog. It just goes to show you make your own karma. Carlos opened his big mouth to hurt others and jeopardize someone's dreams and hopes for the future, and Barney, the dog, opened his mouth to brutally damage Carlos and left a permanent physical scar for the rest of his life.

As the truck rapidly reversed back onto the right track, the sprinklers came on with full force just as the truck did a 360 then purged forward immediately of the property. Rob drove at a deadly pace, trying to avoid getting the powerful spray of the water and getting the truck wet, which could lead to circumstantial evidence. Not a word was spoken by anybody on their return trip. When the small group returned back to the biker property, they unloaded the stolen goods briskly into the sizeable brick shed, not knowing the content contained within. When they finished, they tightly padlocked the large door, and the most supreme high-tech security of that era was switched on.

Rob knocked gently on Emily's door. In a sleepy voice, she called, "Who is it at this hour of the morning?" He explained what had happened to Carlos and asked if she could patch him up. Under no circumstance was he going to a Hospital or doctor's surgery in the local area. Rob apologized for waking her up, as he felt guilty, knowing how she suffered severely from morning sickness all day and night. He had faith in Emily's nursing skills and hoped that she could repair Carlos's foot.

They carried him into the kitchen, his foot bound up in a heavily blood-stained towel. Sitting him in a chair, his lower leg resting on the tabletop, she unravelled the blood-soaked cloth, and Brian nearly fainted at the grotesque sight of his damaged leg and the open wound. He dry reached, and she politely asked Brian to leave the room. Rob changed a paler shade of white and, unable to cope with such a debauched night, left the room. Carlos felt dizzy from such a loss of blood and excruciating pain.

Hastily collecting her thoughts about a plan of action, she raced into the lounge and grabbed a bottle of Incirca Rum. It was 75.9% alcohol and 33% over proof rum. It would make for a primitive anesthetic. She stuck a thick darning needle and some cotton into a small dish of sterile water and placed it in the microwave to boil. This being the only means of sterilization she could think of at the moment. Then, quickly she retrieved it out of the microwave at the ring of its cycle.

Carlos was unsure as to her actions and started to babble on, becoming delirious and semi-conscious. She filled two glasses with the Incirca rum, being extremely potent stuff, and Emily knew one too many drinks of it had been known to kill or leave one unconscious for many hours, then left one with a mighty hangover. Impulsively he sculled the total amount neat, almost instantaneously, falling vaguely into unconsciousness. Emily's time was limited, and she would have to work quickly and precisely, with the sterile tweezers pulling back the torn flesh to reveal as much meat on the inside as she could. With a cotton probe, she douched the wound with antiseptic. Ensuring that it was now a clean, sterile wound, including the surrounding area of the skin she could not afford any infection arising, she began to sew up the deep tear as neatly as possible, praying that it would not turn septic. She then bathed it in a small bowl of saltwater and tea tree oil, which she would continue to do four-hourly for the next forty-eight hours, then clean regularly with colloidal silver to prevent infection. The guys then laid Carlos in his room, where they checked him every couple of hours to ensure he was still alive in the world, knowing Carlos would wake up with a humongous hangover and incredible pain in his lower leg, Emily thought, and as for his foot, well, she felt it was his own fault anyway for the deed he had done.

Rob was pleased that the night was over and at least they had returned home alive, despite the high tension provoked with the group by Carlos's erratic dangerous driving. Rob retired for a few hours of restful sleep and was relieved that the mission had been accomplished but was a little unsure as to how they would go about selling this so-called powerful drug potion. Rob thought he would have to bleed Emily for more information about her friends' intentions concerning the product and how it all worked, even though he knew her loyalty was more toward her newfound friends than his cause.

He would somehow emotionally blackmail her, even though he respected Emily for her commitment and sincerity toward her newfound friends.

It was daybreak. Everybody else retired in one way or another after such a long, arduous night on their mission. Emily, staring out the window out onto the scenic green vines, reminiscing her past as the rain began to beat down on the window. Feelings of forlorn guilt plagued her. Tears started to stream down her face. She felt she had let down the only decent friends she'd ever had in her life and hadn't realized until now how their happiness, laughter, and love had really affected her. And now she missed them terribly, almost experiencing a feeling of homesickness. It had taught her a lesson, though, to appreciate people at the time you are with them, not wait until it's too late. She could foresee their sadness and hopes for their own future destroyed instantly upon returning to find the love potion stolen. Hours later, Rob woke, refreshed from a deep sleep. Wandering out to the shed, overtaken by curiousness, he tore open the lid of one of the large cardboard boxes. On picking up one of the unusually shaped bottles, he broke the seal and removed the cap. Its powerful exotic aroma filled the shed instantly. It made him feel light-headed and caught him off guard as the smell was so sensual he was almost immediately aroused. As he stood up, he accidentally tilted the bottle, spilling quite a large portion of the contents of the perfume bottle. Its aroma was so concentrated, it filled the shed with powerful aromatic strength, wafting out of the small window with the gentle breeze dispersing its fumes across the vast expanse of multiple grapevines.

Back at Fred's Farmhouse, Barney lay on the verandah gloomy. Instantly Barney pricked up his ears and nose, snorting the familiar aroma. Curious, he sniffed the air and began to follow its origin with instinct, the faint scent becoming stronger every step forward on the dirt road. Finally tracking it down after an hour's search finding the smell, he emerged from the large tin shed with slow, deliberate movements, casing the large brick shed, searching intensely for an opening or some way of entering into the building in pursuit of the scent. Stretching up to the window, scratching on the sill, but to no avail did it open. Returning to all fours, the Boxer dog was distracted by Rolf, one of the bikers, who grabbed a wrought iron short rod and hurled it at the Boxer dog. Startled, Barney started to run away. Rolf ran inside and grabbed a gun, quickly loading it up as Barney ran stealthily through the vines. A loud bang penetrated the air, and his legs buckled up beneath him. Barney was killed instantly. As he hit the ground, blood squirted from his head like projectile vomit. His dog spirit left him instantly. Barneys body lay absolutely dead, without a breath of life.

Silence reigned as Rob emerged from the shed. Rob ran to the dead dog. He felt great compassion for the dead animal and a twinge in his heart as he remembered the death of his own beloved dog many years ago. He grabbed Rolf, the dog's murderer, by the scruff of the neck and demanded a reason for such a ruthless action. Rolf was speechless. Rob stared him out in intense passive-aggressive silence, then forcefully pushed him aside, returning to the biker house in silence. Emily was now filled with even more remorse knowing how

Fred loved his Boxer dog Barney, who was now well and truly passed over to the animal spirit world.

Rob made himself a coffee as Emily moved around the kitchen, slowly attending to the domestic chores. Rob realized Emily was upset. He thought she looked so sad and so sweet for such a pregnant little lady. Rob wanted to give her a big hug but stopped himself. What if Brian took offence and presumed the wrong idea. "Why don't you rest, Emily?" he stated. "You work too hard, looking after all of us. Sit down, have a coffee with me. What's on your mind?"

Emily almost burst into tears. She couldn't hold back anymore. Emily told him she was disgusted that he had stolen the powerful drug potion and all her other feelings associated with her newfound friends. She had caught him off guard. He was cross with her stern manner but still proceeded to listen. Once she had started, she couldn't hold herself back from giving out more verbal revilement. He strongly rose up from his seat, exuding an ice coldness from his presence. Emily's voice began to rise immensely. "Anyway," she stated, "the product will never sell because you only have the love potion, and you don't have the rest of the attachments to go with it that will make this gimmick sell." Rob appeared blindsided and confused. "And what's that? What do you mean, love potion? I thought it was some powerful drug potion we could sell on the street?" he said. "The spells, you stupid idiot, it's a love potion perfume." Emily flew out of the kitchen. Running to her room for security, given her outburst, slamming the door shut behind her. He slammed his cup down on the table. Rob suddenly realized he had driven her to go off like she had done. Rob had known Emily for some time now and had never known her to be so loyal to anybody. He wondered momentarily why she felt so strongly about her newfound friends, but he opted to say nothing more about the issue. Besides, Rob didn't want to upset her anymore in her present condition. He sat reflecting, questioning what they had spent the night stealing because if this is not a potent drug potion his biker group can sell, what is it then?

Six

Rob sat in the living room contemplating his next move, his analytical mind racing to devise a way or some plan of hunting down these so-called love spells. The only answer seemed to be to break into Fred's farmhouse again. It would have to be when darkness came, as the following day, the threesome would return home. That night while everybody settled down to sleep, organizing himself by packing a few light significant tools into his backpack, he ventured out into the dark. He walked about a kilometer down the dirt track while walking past the third property, seeing an old pushbike leaning against the tank stand of the small blue-stone cottage. Stealing the bike, he carried it down to the bitumen and cycled in the pitch dark with only the moon shedding any light on the road ahead. As he whizzed past the large gum trees, he stirred up the kookaburras and galas, causing them to disturb the silence of the night. He felt a strange nervousness in his stomach, unusual for him being such a cool character.

He rode the bike almost to the front door of Fred's farmhouse, well aware of Fred's security system and knowing how to dodge the alarms. A chill ran through his blood.

He knew not to break through the front door. It was a most strange feeling he experienced, like someone walked over his grave. The house seemed alive almost. Feeling like he was being watched just like the previous night when he was on his way here to commit the first crime. The feeling stayed haunting him as he continued to proceed. He felt slightly reluctant to enter through the window, but it was too late to back out now. Rob always finished what he started. He stopped instantly, he thought his mind was playing tricks, he thought he saw a moving shadow in the corner then looked again and there was nothing there. He was spooking himself. The air steely.

Climbing through the window, flicking on his torch, he was in the lounge. It was just how Emily had described it. The atmosphere is so cozy. Walking around with such arrogance as if to really make himself at home. Rob was known for his cheek, making a conscious effort not to disturb anything. He crept down the long wide hallway. His pencil torch didn't dispense a great deal of light, and Rob walked straight into a large piece of furniture. He stubbed his toe. "Christ," he muttered as he hobbled on one leg, trying to comfort his injured toe. The shadow in the mirror disappeared suddenly as Rob turned around, grabbing his knapsack, retrieving a larger torch from it, the light quickly flashed against the wall, revealing a face. The visual causes Rob a quick fright. He gasped, then took a deep breath and reassured himself on realizing that it was only a portrait. Rob pointed the torch again in the direction of the picture frame, this time fixed in his tracks. Before him was the face of the most beautiful woman, he had ever seen in his life. Instantly besotted by her beauty, he moved close to stare, touching the picture itself. Her skin looked fresh and aglow with life, her big dark eyes beautiful, full of a wild playful spirit. It lit the flame to his heart. Bewitched by her beauty for a moment. He pulled himself up, returning to reality and to his cause and the job at hand. He could smell the aroma of the love potion emanating from the large antique writing desk. He broke open the roller top draw, trying not to damage it so that no one would notice. There before him was the spell book and a small pouch with Kajo hand-painted on it. He grabbed the articles and put them into his knapsack. He quickly went through all the photographs. In his haste to put them down, his glove caught the corner of one, causing it to fall to the ground. He flashed the torch onto it. It was the same one as on the wall. He wondered if she would miss it but decided to steal it anyway, unable to resist the temptation. His mind could relax now he had achieved his purpose.

Incredibly curious of this enchanted woman, he checked out the rest of the house, unfamiliar mentally with his own tactics. He found her bedroom, having a Japanese-style bed and sensual purple satin sheets which smelt sweetly of Ciniban perfume. The bed was pushed into the corner against the mirror-tiled wall. Plants hung like vines from brass planters and from the top of the black louvred wardrobes. Strewn over the giant peacock chair was such a feminine white lace dress, almost like that of another era. He felt he knew her like he had gone back into another time. He wanted to touch her in real life. The intense passion ignited within him, sitting on the bed, overwhelmed by such a discovery, trying desperately to get a hold of such emotion and withdraw swiftly from intruding into the house. He knew he had to leave immediately. But for some reason, he found it so hard. Overwhelmed by this longing he had never felt in his life before.

A loud thunderous knock on the door brought him swiftly back into reality. He held his breath in fear, thinking whoever was at the door was aware of his existence. Rob could hear heavy footsteps on the verandah. It sounded like two men engrossed in conversation. Once again, another knock. Ducking down quickly to avoid being spotted by the ray of light shining through the window, down on his hands and knees crawling back into the hallway, he clutched his meager belongings, so careful not to make a sound. Momentarily thinking the strangers could hear his heart beating, it pounded so loud within his chest, kneeling on the ground against the wall, listening to their carry-on, hearing a thud on the verandah. Then the strangers' footsteps disappeared, the car doors banging shut, followed by the engine starting up. A blue revolving light turned in silence. Upon realization, it was the Police. He scrambled to hide in the dark corner, not wanting to make a sound to draw any attention that he may be inside the house. Rob sat rigid without moving an inch until he could only hear a very low murmur of the car engine driving off into the dark distance back up onto the main road. Then pulling on his backpack hurriedly, scurrying out of the window, he ran tiptoed across the verandah, almost tripping on the large garbage bag that lay in front of the top step. What was this? he thought, proceeding curiously to check out its contents, holding the small torch in his mouth, to look inside, undoing the knot tied at the end of the giant thick garbage bag.

The foul smell of death hit his nostrils, which went numb

from the disgusting odor. Shining the torch down closer for him to see, then disclosing his find, There staring up at him was the stark cold fixed open eye belonging to Barney, the dead Boxer dog that had been shot the day before on the biker property. Shocked, he ran to the edge of the verandah. Rob couldn't control himself and heaved his guts up straight down into the garden and then tried to hide the vomit with loose garden soil in an effort to cover it up, Turning back in respect, to tie up the large garbage bag with Barney's dead body in it, he was still feeling immensely nauseated. He couldn't seem to move quickly enough to get away from Fred's farm property. Practically jumping on the bicycle like Long John Silver mounts a horse, his legs rotating so fast he almost left the ground on his bike.

Cycling flat out down the road, the smell still strongly lingered in his nose, rushing headstrong into the darkness as he had been gone such a long time. It must have been at least 4:30 a.m. by the time he had returned the stolen bike to its rightful owner and wiped it clean of any fingerprints or traces of its holocene ordeal.

Reverting back home quietly. Slipping in through the large solid oak security door undetected. Rob moving taciturnly into the safety of his own private room, feeling like he needed a shower, yet didn't want to disturb anybody in the household, mainly as Emily's room was situated right next to the bathroom. The death smell still lingered up his nostrils, the faint stench wafting from his black jumper. Pulling it off, throwing it in the corner, he placed an old sheet on top of it in the hope of suffocating the repulsive smell. He turned on his bedside lamp, got into his bed, making himself comfortable, pulling the beautiful picture out of his backpack to revisit the photo. He picked up the photograph of his beauty and held it in his hand, his mind reminiscing his thoughts shot back to her bedroom. He had never had a feeling like it. It was disturbing that he found his mind racing trying to devise ways to meet her in real life. He found himself visualizing little scenarios of them being together without him being a biker or in a different life somehow.

He would investigate and seek out as many details as he could about her from Emily, but he would not in any way disclose his motive. Somehow perhaps he could scheme to meet her and make it look like an accidental meeting. He gently touched the face of the photo. She looked like a real gypsy, with her long burgundy wild tresses. Still, the eyes so profoundly soulful, now feeling terribly guilty about what he had done and understood part of the reason why Emily had become so attached to them. His mind was still racing with his newfound interest, although his body was physically exhausted. Placing the photograph under his pillow, he then fell into a heavy contented sleep. The last three days had indeed been long and definitely eventful. He did, however, feel slightly foolish for mistaking their love potion for a drug potion, and there was a big question as to what he would do with the magical love potion now.

Emily rose early. It was a cleaning day. It appeared that everybody had arisen already and had gone their own ways for the day. She thought it was the ideal opportunity to vacuum the house, her hands darting back and forth, sweeping every-thing in sight. She wiped down the corridor, knocking Rob's door ajar. She ventured in, then suddenly realized he lay in his bed sound asleep. She quickly turned off the noise. She heard a slight flutter and thought she must have disturbed something. Quickly and cautiously bending down to retrieve it, she almost gasped. It was a photo of Kaitlin. Placing it face down and back on the floor, she removed herself promptly from the room before being discovered. Secretly wondering what his intentions were, she hoped he was not premeditating any physical harm to Kaitlin.

Half sleepy-eyed, Rob staggered into the kitchen, wearing only his scrubbed denim jeans. His body was tanned and taut, Emily for a second, admiring his body. Thinking to herself that it could never be denied, he was pretty sexy. He sat there eating his muesli, the sun streaming through the window, assessing his goals mentally for the day. Rob had to check on the crops of dope today. They were so close to maturity, soon having to be hung and dried out in the large shed where the boxed love potion was currently housed. Today, he would feed the plants adequate amounts of fish emulsion to make their resin strong, giving the plants a good head to help them along with a quicker maturity date.

"Emily," he inquired. "What's Kaitlin like?" "Why do you ask?" defensive she asked? "Because I'm curious why you care so much about your friendship with her, Jo and Fred," he said. Emily described Kaitlin as a beautiful, warm, spiritual, mystical, loving being with very high moral standards, generously caring towards others, and fun-loving. Still, deep down, she has never gotten over her fiancee. "So they split?" he inquired. "No, he died in a motorbike accident," she stated. "So was he a biker?"

Rob sounded more curious than ever. "No way. He was

a lawyer. Apparently, they absolutely adored each other. In fact, from what I have seen, his photograph looks similar to you. except he was a much warmer personality and very polite type, without the gross beard." On the sarcastic statement from Emily, Rob looked at her with a distinct hurt in his eyes, even though he tried to hide it. At times her words were so cutting and blunt, they almost stuck into him like a knife. She really did have a way of getting to him, maybe because she was a woman who was so brutally honest. He really didn't want to be such a bastard at times, but to maintain his leadership in the biker gang and complete this drug deal, he had to hide behind his superficial image, it was necessary to be like that until the right time came. He sat in deathly quiet at the table, sipping his coffee, and looked away from her, deep in his own thoughts, knowing no one can fool anyone better than one can fool themselves at times. Secretly if Emily knew what he was really like, she would never have made such a comment. Rob sat, very curt with a fixed, intense stare regarding Emily as she continued to wash the dishes, Rob snapped back." Well, anyway, I was only asking."

Emily leaned across the table, pushing down on her frail hands, staring him straight in the eye with a threatening voice. "If you in any way physically harm Kaitlin, I will per-sonally kill you, no matter what it costs." He had never seen Emily so determined, replying that wasn't his intention and she should just chill. She was causing herself a lot of undue stress. Emily made a subconscious promise she would keep a close eye on Rob from now on and be right behind him, watching constantly.

Seven

The threesome sat contented as Fred drove at a healthy speed to get home early before sundown. It had been a most eventful three days and they were all enthused. They had met so many people and had felt all their long hard hours putting the project together had met with great praise and would all be worthwhile. They may not necessarily make a million from the first contract discussed in one of their meetings with a potential buyer. Still, once Jo and Kaitlin divided the profits, it would give them each a substantial amount of money to pursue their own careers and interests without having to do so much nursing. Fred was similar in attitude to Wally, just an all-out good guy who had thoroughly enjoyed just being along for the ride and wanted to see Jo and Kaitlin be successful.

As Kaitlin sat observing the scenery out the window watching Fred drive, she was deep in thought, thinking how sweet Jo and Fred looked together as Jo sleeping huddled up next to him on the front seat. Kaitlin started getting rather cold, thinking, at times like this, she really missed Dave. Kaitlin missed the affection that one could have in a relationship. Drifting back now, thinking how nice it would be to have a shower and get into bed to get some rest, she was utterly exhausted. They hadn't slept much over the last few days. Maybe they could grab some Chinese food on the way home, as she couldn't be bothered to cook dinner. She asked Fred to make a short detour to the Chinese shop for some food.

Fred pulled in and went into the Chinese shop. Jo and Kaitlin sat outside in the car. A strange feeling passed through Kaitlin, who spoke her thoughts out aloud to Jo "I hope every-thing's all right at home. I feel like someone just walked over my grave. How strange." Jo replied, "It scares me when you get those feelings, Kaitlin," said Jo. "Me too," replied Kaitlin. Nothing more was said, and they munched into dinner like three ravaged seagulls, receiving their first meal in days. Back on the road now, Fred continued to drive only a couple of kilometers away. They were all happy and grateful that the journey would soon be over, Fred wearily pulling up into the driveway, which looked so inviting. All three bailed out of the car. Being first up on to the verandah, Fred stood like a monument of stone, stopping dead in his tracks. That strange shudder passed up Kaitlin's spine again. Fred warned Jo and Kaitlin to pass by the bag, unsure about its contents and told the two ladies to go inside and not be so inquisitive. Fred could hardly stand the smell. On undoing the bag, he let out a loud pang of hysteria.

He ran into Jo, yelling, "It's Barney. It's Barney." Jo was startled at his behavior. He grabbed onto her. "He's dead, Jo. He's dead." Fred was emotionally beside himself. Jo said nothing and just hugged him as silent tears swelled up in her eyes.

She just let him release the emotion and tried to comfort him. Fred went to the bedroom, being so upset. When you lose a pet, you have almost had a lifetime. It's such a devastating feeling. One never forgets, and you only know that type of pain if you have experienced it first hand. In the quiet of his bedroom, Fred cried bitterly. About an hour later, Jo came out of the bedroom and made him a cup of tea. In the kitchen, the two young women promptly decided that it would be a good idea to bury the dog in a special dog funeral fashion. Kaitlin reassured Jo to go back in and comfort Fred. She would sort something out for a proper burial for Barney. Although having endured a long journey and being totally buggered from the last three days' events, Kaitlin pressed on to prepare something for Barney, motivating herself by the fact that that's what friends are for, to help you out in your hour of need. Besides, thought Kaitlin, they helped her out when David died.

The sunset, sending off magnificent rays of mauve and pink across the sky. Kaitlin shovelled a large hole in the ground next to the old gum tree at the side of the house, covering her hands with gloves, picking up the heavy bag, putting it into the hole, the dead-smelling carcass made her dry reach profusely, but it was a job that had to be done. Hurriedly she covered the bag with the rich garden soil which was becoming so fly blown. When it was fully covered over, she made a large cross out of twigs and stuck it on top of the grave, then sat there for a moment wondering who would do such a cruel thing. The three would have to report the incident to the Police, but not right now. It was best to sleep on it and talk to Fred once he had a little time to digest Barneys' death.

Up at the crack of dawn, keenly motivated was Kaitlin. Anxiously opening the shed door to once again inhale their excellent love potion, only to behold before her the sight of the large cement floor empty and cold with all the magical love potion disappeared into thin air. What had gone on while they had been away? This sure felt weird. Was this some type of joke on them? This needed to be investigated. Kaitlin was intent on finding out who had jeopardized their territory and their future. Mentally debating if the criminal was aware he was definitely playing with fire. Her immediate thoughts were of total revenge, but how can you revenge a culprit when you don't know who it was or why, plus no matter how you feel, what's the point? Two wrongs don't make a right. But she would get to the bottom of it.

Jo appeared out from nowhere and entered the sizeable empty shed. Kaitlin looked at her but said nothing. Jo's mouth dropped with bitter disappointment. Almost hitting the floor, she sat down next to Kaitlin on the big wooden crate. What had they done to deserve so much crap in the last twenty-four hours? Jo began to cry. She ventured back into the farmhouse and down the wide hallway, saddened at the find and wondering what to do or say to Fred, whom she had left to sleep and recover from the emotional shock of the significant loss of his beloved Barney. Jo and Kaitlin sat in the kitchen discussing tactics, deciding there was no other alternative but to go to the Police. Kaitlin made a list of questions.

Fred entered the kitchen wearily. Both the girls looked at him with such sad facial expressions. He knew something was amiss. Jo broke the news. Fred ran down to the shed and checked it out for himself. He checked his surveillance. There was nothing, not a trace of anything. He punched the wall, leaving a permanent dent, swearing profusely with intent to destroy the person responsible for their loss. Jo and Kaitlin left him in the shed until he calmed down, then he came back, entering the kitchen to collect the car keys. Jo and Kaitlin informed Fred that they were all going to the Police now. Climbing in the car's driver's seat, Fred drove angrily as the girls held on tightly to their seats. Fred drove at speed not typical to his usual cautious self. Then Kaitlin demanded he pull over, and then she drove. Kaitlin pulled up with an abrupt halt out front of the Police Station. Fred opened the car door for Jo and Kaitlin and gently but sternly advised them that he would do all the talking. He seemed more in control now. Thank God, it was unusual to see him like this. But no matter how passive a person can be, everybody has a breaking point, and when it goes, it can be with an almighty snap.

They entered the Police Station. It had such a staid atmosphere. Fred almost had a mental blank as the huge overweight Police Officer asked him what he wanted in his slow ocker drawl. His appearance being crass, Kaitlin wondered how he would go chasing after an offender. Jo and Kaitlin must have been thinking exactly the same as they both looked at each other when he spoke so crassly to them, and both Jo and Kaitlin fought hard to retain their composure. Although the Police Officer wasn't quick enough to pick up on what they thought, Fred explained how they had returned to find the Boxer dog shot dead and bagged up, and their house was broken into, And all their product for sale, had been stolen. The Police Officer filled him in on the basic facts regarding his Boxer dog. Stating that it had been found by one of the workers on a block a couple of kilometres from Fred's property. The Police Officer wouldn't give out names and gave out as little information as possible.

Fred, becoming defensive, demanded more explanation, needing to know where the animal was found, as he wanted to find Barney's gold collar, being a valuable item and mainly for sentimental purposes. One of the other Police Officers sympathized, innocently volunteering the information much to the Sergeant's disgust, although no verbal comment was made.

The three walked outside of the Police Station. Uttering not a word until out of earshot and climbing into the car. Jo sat bolt upright in the car and turned to look at Kaitlin. "Are you thinking what I'm thinking?"

"I certainly am," replied Kaitlin, who then ordered Fred to drive just down the road a short way and hide the car amongst the trees. While briefly planning their tactics, they then ran through the scrub, bending down quickly and quietly, moving unnoticed around the back of the Police Station, keeping very low, removing even their shoes so as not to make a sound. The three crouched in single file, near the open window. Sneaking ever so cautious. Pinning their ears as close as they dared beneath the open window. Listening intently to the big Police Officer spill his guts over the phone. His conversation was such that it was clear he was somehow involved in this little racket. Kaitlin, Jo and Feed, having heard enough, sneaked away, swiftly back to the car to prevent being caught in the act. On jumping in the car, out of earshot, they verbally abused the big Police Officer until the anger was channeled out of their systems. As the old saying goes, you make your own Karma. The Police Officer would get his, and from the look on Fred's face, it would probably be very soon. They just had to do this in the right way, so it was not detrimental to their lives.

Jo returned from work the next day, laughing so hardy, divulging that the Police Officer had walked out onto his home front verandah that next morning in the process of heading off to work. While stepping on the old wooden stairs, unfor-tunately, all his weight had gone right through the wooden stairs. He had fallen to the ground, broken his leg, torn all the ligaments in his knee cap, and needed a total knee recon-struction. Fred laughed. Fred, with a twinkle in his eye, said, "There you go, Kaitlin. You were right. You certainly do make your own Karma." Jo and Kaitlin knew he had something to do with that but didn't dare ask. Fred laughed aloud. He had hoped for such a good result as he had sawed away at the old wood the previous night and covered it over by making it appear to be an accident. Fred never ever mentioned that situation again, nor did anyone else ever ask.

Eight

Two days later, Fred was fired up and set about hunting down Barney's gold dog collar using his gold metal detector. Eventually, after a couple of persistent hours or so of searching around the closest farm properties, Fred finally came across it, appearing only half visible from being buried in the dirt amongst the grapevines. Picking it up, he felt a pang of sadness, missing his beloved Barney dearly, reflecting momentarily, recalling so many of the good times together, especially when Fred was younger. Barney always seemed to be around when he was going through his painful teenage years. Fred knew this sadness. Barney was quietly supportive, understanding and gave him all the unconditional love any man could ever want. Fred squatted there, holding the collar in deep sentiment, then on inhaling the fresh air, realized he had smelt that faint unforgettable aroma of their magical love potion. Standing up, looking around, trying to determine from which direction it had come, not far from where Fred was standing 200 meters away was an oversized brick garage. Venturing nearer, he felt assured that there wasn't anybody in the surrounding vicinity.

As Fred neared the shed, the air became thick with the scent of the magical love potion perfume. Searching for an opening but unable to enter the shed as it was heavily padlocked and the security tight, he walked to the side of it. On coming across a small window, Fred peered in through its dusty pane. There it was to his surprise all the boxes in tact and the aroma emanating strongly out the window. He was ecstatic about finding the location of the magical love potion. Desperately retaining his excitement, as he was about to run back home, Fred stopped suddenly, crouching down quickly, hiding behind a beaten up old unused tractor that stood very close to the shed.

The local Police Officer had arrived, knocking on the door of the house across the way. A young man appeared at the front door. They both walked from the house to the shed. Rob unlocked the shed door, and they entered. The Police Officer, aghast by the fumes, asked Rob to open the window. Fred almost panicked when the window flew open, thinking he had been discovered but relieved to know this was not so. Fred slightly unnoticed moved back over underneath the window to see if he could hear what they were talking about. Fred was fortunate enough to hear the conversation very clearly. It definitely appeared that the Police Officer with the broken leg, and the other young Police Officer were tied up with this crew of gangsters and involved in a huge drug ring. The Police Officer wanted to know when the drug crop would be ready to be sold. Rob sounded almost reluctant to divulge any information, but really he wasn't entirely with the conversation. Since he had come across Kaitlin's photo, his whole attitude and some of his pre-set goals had begun to change.

Rob had almost lost sight of his present aim, in fact now he was questioning his whole existence. Amazingly, the influence one can have on people at certain times in one's life can come out of left field. It can be at a time when one may least expect it, and sometimes that's when one can be most vulnerable. That's just part of the magical excitement life has to offer. Rob and the Police Officer discussed their business briefly, the two then parting, and the Police Officer leaving the property. Rob returned to the biker's house, realizing he had only vaguely been aware of the conversation. His mind is so preoccupied with devising some way of meeting Kaitlin.

As soon as the scene was safe, Fred scurried home, charging quickly through the grapevines and across the paddocks. It was the fastest he had run in a long time, the run almost leaving him breathless, but unfortunately, Fred had returned home to an empty house. Jo and Kaitlin had gone into town to do the weekly shopping. Caught up in his own tangent. Forgetting the fact that they went shopping at this same time every Friday. Emily asked Rob to take her into town, needing some goods from the chemist. Plus, she had to pick up some raspberry tea from the health shop, drinking enormous amounts religiously to ward off her morning sickness, adopting the idea from a book of one of Kaitlin's old herb remedies. Rob reluctantly drove her into town in the small van, which they used communally for specific outings.

While Emily was busy in the supermarket, she suddenly spotted Jo and Kaitlin, feeling slightly guilty but pleased to see them. Emily rushed up and threw her arms around them both so tightly, almost zapping them of energy. Emily felt a sudden rush of emotion, but in her very conservative way, retained it all. They chatted briefly, giggling merrily, and then parted.

Jo and Kaitlin walked outside the store to load the car up with the groceries. Emily surveyed the supermarket, looking for Rob, who had somehow disappeared just before she had run into Jo and Kaitlin. Emily went out to the van where Rob had his head stuck behind an open newspaper. As she stepped into the Van, she could see that he wore an incredibly guilty look on his face. "Serves yourself right," she said. Emily was starting to become rather cheeky lately. He didn't like her attitude or snide remark. Nothing more was said. Rob sat there staring as the two emerged from the store once again. Emily stared at him and saw a warm glow creep across his face. His eyes lit up, and his head veered slightly forward. Emily knew then that, in actual fact, he had fallen in love with Kaitlin and now could understand his strange behavior over the last few days. She was glad that at least he could have feelings for someone even if, in her opinion, he had Buckley's chance of ever getting to know Kaitlin.

Kaitlin and Jo started to walk toward them. Rob thought, what a beautiful creature, and he was aware that most of the people had noticed and turned to look twice to admire her beauty. Suddenly he started up the engine of the van and took off swiftly. Rob realized they were walking toward the truck to speak with Emily. He turned on the engine of the van then made a swift turn, and the two ladies were left behind. Taking off recklessly, Emily clung securely to her safety belt and didn't ask for an explanation of his actions. It was necessary to take this course of action. He didn't want Kaitlin to think he was a no-hoper. He simply didn't want to meet her yet.

"Did you know they would be here?" he asked Emily. "I didn't really think about it, actually. They shop here every Friday at this time," she replied. Slyly, out of the corner of his eye, Rob craftily checked his watch for the time, mentally taking note to remember it. Rob and Emily drove home calmly, Emily unaware that she had just accidentally leaked some vital information. Now he could plan some course of action, having something more substantial to work from. Rob distracting Emily swapped subjects asking if Brian would be back before dark as he was aware Brian had been working out of the parameters of the biker property today checking and repairing all the fences "Yes he does work hard." agreed Rob. Emily piped up again defensive "Yes and lets hope he gets paid for all the hard work he does do."

Nine

On their return trip, Jo and Kaitlin were stunned. Happy and angry to find out what Fred had to say as he divulged his discovery of where the magical love potion was located. Suspiciously, Jo actually did wonder now if Emily had anything to do with the magical love potion theft. Kaitlin was sitting on the fence with this without making a judgement until she knew the facts, as she felt when the two were in town grocery shopping, it was almost as if Emily was trying to tell them something. Jo had fired so many questions at her it was ten to the dozen on so many subjects, leaving Emily no chance to explain or even answer half of the questions. Now the three realized they were in a compromised situation, knowing the local Police were also possibly involved in the heist of the magical love potion. Kaitlin still could not understand why someone would want to steal the magical love potion in the first place. The three would really have to think carefully and devise an excellent plan of recuperating the love potion. The biggest problem would be taking the blame and finger-pointing away from them, and also, it would have to be a rock-solid swift act so they wouldn't incriminate themselves and get caught. Kaitlin sitting down at the big square kitchen table, said to Jo and Fred, "If we were going to try and retrieve our magical love potion back, how would we do that?" Fred replied brashly, "I am pretty sure it's called theft, Kaitlin." She looked at him whimsically. Jo quietly laughed, then piped up, saying, "I have never stolen anything, so I don't know what to do, even though it belongs to us. Why would the Police want to steal our magical love potion? Do you think the Police Officer is addicted to the magical love potion? Fred playfully replied, "Now there's a thought".

Kaitlin serious spoke, "Somehow we could make it look like some sort of an accident, but it would have to be so frightening it would rid the town of the bikers for good, so they would never be a threat to the three of us ever." Fred butted in, "Exciting!! And so sinister Kaitlin, wow, I wouldn't want to cross you. The question is how to do it?" The three sat silent for a moment. It was indeed a challenge, although it was annoying to all three knowing that they had to even contemplate such an act. "How's that for justice? Said Jo loudly. They continued discussing working out a plan while getting on with life for the next week to develop a steely realistic strategy.

Meanwhile, out on his investigative mission, Rob returned to the biker property, quietly organizing himself. On going to his bedroom, Rob packed some of his good quality clothes into his rucksack, letting Emily know he would be away for three days. Then Rob drove through the small township out past Kaitlin's property and on to the next farming town, which was about fifteen kilometers, far enough not to be discovered by anyone else in the biker group, close enough to Kaitlin. In this new town, he would hide his identity and appear to be a totally different character, and living a very different life.

Rob booked into the local hotel, which lay on the outskirts of town. The Publican seemed instead a helpful friendly chap, inviting Rob into the front bar for a beer. Declining the offer momentarily, Rob reassured him he would be down for a beer and chat in a couple of hours. Once in his room, Rob hurriedly unpacked his clothes, ensuring they were clean and well pressed. He took a long refreshing shower, then decided upon a shave, which revealed in the mirror those handsome spic and span features that used to run his father's million-dollar business. Rob thought his vocabulary may have slipped but prized himself on his brain, still being very astute. He applied Drake Moi Aftershave, which he brought from the chemist shop that morning, knowing via Emily that it was Kaitlin's favorite, hoping he had remembered the right name from one of Emily's brief statements of Kaitlin's taste.

Rob thought aloud, "Anyway, enough of this vain admiring himself in the mirror business. Let's get organized." There was little time and so much to do. He needed a haircut. Stepping from his room looking so totally different, dressed in a grey-flecked double-breasted suit, white shirt, and black leather tie. His new image certainly didn't suit his motor biker life, although somehow it would have to do temporarily until he got to the next step. Walking down the main street to the closest hairdressers he could find off-the-main road for a ten-minute haircut. Rob bundled himself into the barbershop. He took a seat in the warm, friendly barbers shop, although there was no one else in there at the time. The lovely young girl explained that her boss had gone out to one of the farms to help his mate with his overladen grape picking crops. As time was of the essence, he took a risk and had her cut his hair, and she had done an excellent job cutting and styling Rob's hair. He now looked so different with this last stage of the makeover. She commented how good-looking he was. Flirting with him, then even asked him for a date. Declining the offer graciously, he had his mission to think of. He inquired if there was a car hiring service in the town. She gladly offered her advice and informed him that there was a rent-a-car truck service at the end of the main street. Rob was clearly happy as all these things were coming together so quickly. So far, so good, he thought.

He asked for the best deal for a week and signed up instantly, and chose a decent executive type car. He decided to use his father's charge account card to obtain the rental vehicle on this occasion. It would probably be six months before his father even noticed, Secretly hoping his prediction would be correct, and he would think of a valid excuse as to why he had done this, that was if his father even asked him to explain at a later date. Very happy, he returned to the hotel for a counter tea, and a chat with the local Publican, whom he was sure would fill him in on all the local gossip and details of who was who in the area and where to get the best deal on things you needed. The Publican seemed to take a shining to Rob. He thought him very much a city slicker and recognized him from some of the society pages, much to Rob's disliking. It just goes to show, no matter how much you try to hide it, your reputation follows you everywhere. The Publican being rather proud to have Rob in his establishment, the two chatted about the footy for a while. Then he inquired why Rob was staying in town. Rob was momentarily caught off guard, unsure what to say, then somehow diverted the conversation back to the Publican and how he came to own the hotel. Rob listened enthusiastically for a long time.

On quickly glancing at an advertisement on the wall regarding writing, it seemed an appropriate answer to use. Rob replied at the appropriate time, "I'm writing a novel." He hated lying. He was the worst liar and almost felt like retrieving his statement, as he was tripping over his words, but it was too late. The Publican was in awe and had no reason not to believe Rob. Knowing the old cliche, if you make your bed, you have to lie in it, then sadly, Rob knew he would have to tell more lies to cover himself. Rob tried to fade out of the conversation and let the Publican do most of the talking, assuring himself mentally that he was telling lies for self-protection only. No point in stewing on it. The Publican inquired as to where he would be staying. Rob hadn't thought that far ahead yet. The Publican replied, "I've got the perfect place for you if you want to get away by yourself to write. A friend of mine has got a little old house about five kilometres out of town. Would you like me to ring her for you? I'll put the good word in for ya." Rob was taken by the opportunity. And nodded his head to agree.

Rob sat patiently at the bar, sipping his beer, slowly awaiting the Publican's return. The prominent Publican talked on the phone in a friendly fashion and organized the accommodation all for him. So far, he'd had such luck, he wondered what the farm would be like, how interesting. It was a good break and would enable him to get his next move organized.

It's like everything, though. It's just a matter of being in the right place at the right time.

That night on retiring to bed, he felt very confident with his present situation. It was nice to get away and be the person he really was without being inhibited. He pulled out Kaitlin's photo from his wallet, staring at it in deep adoration. He kissed it and placed it under the pillow and, wafting off into the realms of deep sleep, wishing her a peaceful goodnight.

He rose early, doing his regular sit-ups to keep his body trim, taut, and in shape. He dressed, ate breakfast, and was off to the local bank. In his account was deposited thousands of dollars. He then went to buy some jeans, sandshoes, denim shirts, long-sleeve tee shirts, and a denim jacket. It had been a long time since he had bought himself some clothes and for-gotten the thrill and the fun one could have with retail ther-apy. It can undoubtedly raise self-esteem. Almost strutting down the street, there was a definite air of distinction about him. He only hoped that it would do the trick. He thought of Kaitlin, experiencing a certain nervousness in his guts. He could have mistaken it for excitement. He wasn't sure, but it was foreign, like nothing he had experienced before. He hadn't wasted any time with his shopping, and he was back at the Hotel by lunchtime. He entered the lounge bar to check with the Publican about the tiny house to rent.

This was when he met Rosie, What an experience. Rosie was a big Fraulein woman, with the accent to match. She seemed kindhearted enough but was the type who always had to be shoving food in your mouth, thinking that was the way to make people feel at home. He realized she meant well, although slightly irritated with her arrogant but amicable manner. Rob thought it worth his while for the eventual outcome, especially if it meant that he could rent out that particular house, be completely elusive, and hideaway away from prying eyes. He didn't want to blow his chances or put a spanner in the works, so to speak. Rob prayed she wouldn't be continuously annoying him once he settled in. The lest people he had to talk to, the better he thought.

Rosie and Rob drove out to the property. To Rob's surprise, it was great and met with his satisfaction, everything in order and meticulously clean, the mezzanine floor so polished you could eat a meal of it. But most Europeans are known for their cleanliness. Rosie had even set up a large wooden table in the comer near the window for him to write on. She seemed like she was good at organizing everybody's life, but he didn't seem to mind under the circumstances. It was one of the rare occasions that he chose not to say anything. Maybe he was maturing with his age, or perhaps he had become more tolerable.

Who cares anyway? Life is too short to argue. The place was much to his requirement. She ordered him to upkeep the garden, water the indoor plants, and keep the area clean. The rest was his business. He paid his minimal rent, and as he watched her drive off down the dirt track, he thought, what a dominating woman, and wondered what sort of a relationship the Publican and her really had. People's lives can be so interesting. They seemed happy together. Well, that's the main thing, really, isn't it? Rob thought to himself as he wandered around the compact house, looking over everything again. Did this suit his purpose? Did this suit his new image? Well, it would have to do.

Kaitlin would have to like it. He loved the kitchen. It looked highly wholesome and would look even better once he had been to the health shop and bought ample healthy food supplies. It would be good to be back into his own cooking and decent food. Although Emily's cooking was delicious, she couldn't cook vegetarian like him. Well, so he thought, anyway. He would have to get the shopping done in a hurry. His time was limited. He would have to organize a typewriter, although Rosie had mentioned she had one he could borrow. He may take up the option. After all, it would save him money. Besides, one should never look a gift horse in the mouth.

Tools he would definitely require were writing paper and pens. He wanted his impression to be professional. Taking time out, he took out Kaitlin's photo and sat rocking in the old hand-carved wooden rocking chair. He wondered if she would even like him and hoped that this effort had not been in vain. He would hate to have premeditated something that would just turn out a disaster, but he reassured himself with deep-seated confidence and wondered why it felt so right. But to reach a goal, one must believe in oneself, for only then is it possible.

He tried his new clothes on, admiring himself in the mirror. Not bad, he thought, with a slight chuckle, suddenly realizing the time. He had a lot to accomplish now, having to drive back into town, hire a trailer, and bring out his motorbike and help the Publican with a few little chores. After all, he thought, it doesn't hurt to do someone a good deed. The motorbike could be stored in the shed out of sight, enabling him to ride back to the biker property in the early hours of the morning and check that the biker gang was doing their job correctly in conjunction with the drug crop time line. It was a crucial time, as the drug crop was almost ready, and he was making sure that he was keeping a tight reign on his produce. He didn't trust some of those guys, especially where drugs were involved. He now decided to spend very late afternoons and nights at the biker farm. If all went well. He locked the door of his new little abode, stepping out, feeling smug about his secret Idaho.

Dressed in new denim jeans, a blue denim shirt, and white sandshoes, he felt good, like a casual yuppie. He drove into town. While there, it seemed as good a time as any to purchase some groceries for his holiday. Browsing around the health food shop, it had been a while since he had entered one. That old familiar clean smell of oats, bran-made bread and spinach rolls mingled through the air. He took his time to shop, loading himself up with plenty of goods. The shelves were slightly restricting as they were placed close together. He emptied his load onto the bench to go through the checkout. The chap serving seemed a somewhat spiritual soul and very friendly. The atmosphere was relaxed, as Rob was the only customer in the shop. He then remembered he would need some wholemeal corn flour. Dashing back around the row of shelves situated down the center of the shop, almost knocking into them with his shoulder, he hurried so as not to keep the chap waiting, grabbing the larger two-kilogram bag. That would save him having to come back for a while. Briskly walking around down the aisle, as he sharply turned the corner of the shelves, he ran straight into a woman. Startled by her presence, he dropped the bag of cornflour, which splattered all over the floor, raising a great cloud of dust. He immediately apologized.

She stood motionless, mesmerized as if she had been thrust back into the past. Feeling as if there was a ghost before her. She turned a white shade of grey for a moment. Then shook her head to bring herself back into reality. Touching his sleeve, she replied, almost laughing, "That's okay, but we had better clean it up." Still, she was unsure if this was for real or whether it was just her wild imagination running away with itself again. The chap who owned the shop laughed at the situation but proceeded to sweep up the mess with the broom, reassuring them not to worry about it. No point in worrying about such a trivial matter. The shopkeeper would fix it up.

Rob offered to pay for the damage, but the chap wouldn't hear of it. "Why don't you just buy the little lady a cup of dandelion coffee? I'll make it especially for you. Just take a seat over near the window." Rob, unable to refuse the shopkeeper, was rather amused, and the shop owner's observation told him he had just witnessed the meeting of twin flames. The shopkeeper felt the electrical energy when the two had banged into each other, although the shopkeeper wasn't sure if the two of them knew that yet. Rob hadn't really bargained for this meeting and was totally caught off guard. Trying to hold himself back from becoming too involved in the conversation, through fear of putting her off, thinking to himself how beautiful she was in real life, dressed in her cheesecloth gypsy skirt, and little top that laced up down the front, her hair wild, long, and vivacious.

This, to Kaitlin, was an unexpected situation. Feeling as

though she owed him an explanation, although not wanting to spoil such luck, Kaitlin introduced herself while enjoying the coffee and thanked him for it, inquiring about his name so she could address the guy adequately.

"Do you live around here?" His reply was no, explaining that he was only visiting the area. Her curiousness got the better of her, wanting to know how long he was staying for, sensing that he was a little reluctant to offer any information and very reserved.

Kaitlin, not wanting to appear totally nosy, changed the course of the conversation. Unable to hold back anymore, she just had to explain her feelings, remarking, "I feel like I've known you for years." He too stated, "It's funny you should say that because I really do feel the same way," he replied.

That remark filled her with a warm sensation. Kaitlin was a little confused, whether it was because his personal appearance was almost identical to her darling deceased David, who had passed away in a fatal motorbike accident, or whether it was just Rob's animal magnetism and personality that attracted her. Strangely enough, he became more relaxed, disclosing why he had come to this little country town. Kaitlin was thrilled that he was a writer and explained that one of her future ambitions and dreams was similar. The idea had to be put aside for the moment, as she was working to pursue such an interest with writing but in a different sense. Rob asked Kaitlin where she lived, although secretly knowing full well. She explained that she lived about ten kilometers down the road and had only come into this township to visit the dentist, as that particular dentist was the best in the area, and usually, she didn't come into this town. She generally shopped in Cobdobla and thought it would be a good idea to check out the health shop for a few odds and ends while here in the small town. They both chatted away profusely for quite a long time. It was soon time for the shopkeeper to close, so they would have to leave. Rob still had to organize his motorbike, so he explained that he had to go and left on an enjoyable note.

Kaitlin, didn't want him to leave and really didn't want to let him go, but that's life. As he paid the shopkeeper, Rob thanked him. The shopkeeper winked with a bit of twinkle in his eye. Rob actually beamed a radiant smile. Only turning to catch a glimpse of the shopkeeper's fading smile, they then left the shop. Kaitlin tried to keep him talking even though she knew he had to go. Rob bid her farewell and walked away with an incredible feeling of being elated. Kaitlin felt like her heart started to sink but couldn't understand such a reaction. Watching him walk to his car and get in, Kaitlin turned to walk down the street toward her car. As she was about to climb into the car, someone grabbed her arm gently from behind, pleasantly surprised, it was Rob again. He was almost nervous asking her, as he was not used to asking women out at all. They usually asked him out. Kaitlin was secretly thrilled by such a chivalrous display. He asked her if she would like to have dinner with him. Accepting his invitation immediately, they exchanged phone numbers. Kaitlin softly bid him farewell, then jubilantly driving off in the car, overwhelmed by the whole scenario.

This really was too good to be true, wondering if all the decrees and affirmations that she had repeatedly chanted in the last few months had now manifested into the physical reality and had drawn a soul mate to her. Still wondering if this man who had entered her life was aware of the cosmic forces that seemed to be happening. Maybe Kaitlin was kidding herself. Perhaps it was only she who felt this way and saw the situation through rose-colored glasses. Hopefully not as she double guessed herself. Maybe he had felt something, reassuring herself that he would not have asked for a dinner date if he wasn't interested in her. If only she knew what he was thinking. Maybe Kaitlin would indeed be surprised if she really knew the truth. Her analytical mind worked overtime. What would she wear? What would be suitable? He appeared to be immaculately dressed even though he was in casual clothes. The feeling of excitement surged through her blood. It was the first time in a long while, and it was certainly unusual for Kaitlin to be falling for someone at first sight. As usual, her efficient and logical mind took over when it came to affairs of the heart. Maybe she was throwing caution to the wind. It was too late anyway. She was already involved and had no intentions of backing out of the date. She needed to know more about him and what he was really like.

Rob couldn't believe his luck. He felt ecstatic. What a meeting. He must have been riding the wave of good luck. His last forty-eight hours had produced some great results and ones that were truly unexpected. He quickly organized a hire trailer, returned to the Hotel, thanked the Publican for his help and for letting him store the motorbike in his garage. he loaded it onto the trailer. He secured it with ropes, ensuring in the process that he didn't mark or scratch his beast of a magnificent machine and beloved prize beauty. Driving back to his little hideaway, unsure of the future, locking up the motorbike in the very clean rear shed. He covered it with an old black sheet. The hut was in a good position, being situated at the rear of the house very undetected. Cooking himself a very healthy meal, when on contemplation, his appetite had already disappeared. His mind was preoccupied. He hoped he hadn't made a wrong impression on such a well-together woman. He was not at all surprised by her warm, intelligent nature. The situation had totally caught Rob off guard. He felt foolish about dropping the cornflour but now managed to find it rather amusing. He hadn't felt so inwardly happy in years. But the question of why, still bubbled at the surface of his thoughts? No one had ever captivated him this way in his life.

On Kaitlin's return, Jo and Fred had been worried and inquired why the journey had taken so long. When she was explaining what happened, they both seemed rather pleased and were happy for her.

Jo said, "It's about time you had that little twinkle back in your eye. It seems to have faded lately, especially since our magical love potion disappeared." Knowing Kaitlin had become so discouraged at the inhumanity of the incident and had tried not to think of the significant loss. Still, she knew they would have to sit down and contemplate the next move and some action before it was too late, and they would lose all hope of regaining the magical love potion.

Ten

Kaitlin's mind was racing thinking how they could retrieve the magical love potion, analyzing the analyses, coming up with various ideas on some decent sort of strategy. Maybe she could revert to a movie concept and apply an idea out of a horror movie instead of thinking of a realistic plan. Perhaps they could somehow use a vision based on witchcraft, using some sort of fake apparition, and try and scare the culprits. Relieved that the day's work was finished, Kaitlin had been working at the country Hospital as of late. It seemed like it had been such a long day, although parts of the day having held a reasonable amount of interest especially with a few babies that had been delivered. Kaitlin had watched the clock tick on all day. Returning home, heading straight for the kitchen, Tonight Kaitlin's appetite was incredible as her stomach had been abandoned since meeting with Rob. Jo, Fred, and Kaitlin drank their coffee, discussing a few more possibilities on how they could steal back the love potion. They laughed so hardily at some of the outlandish ideas they come up with.

Fred was very serious suddenly about the issue as he didn't

want the two girls to be put in any horrific situation. His impression of what some bikers would do to a woman was probably to the extremes of dramatic, and he was very protective toward the two. They feared that harm would come to them and knew that it would have to be a dynamic plan, mostly carried out by him, otherwise, he would not have been able to live with himself if something terrible happened to Jo or Kaitlin. Honestly, it was somewhat mentally draining, and they racked their brains intensely. Jo joking stated it was the first time in a while that her brain had had to work so hard because being so carefree, she looked upon it with a thrill-seeker attitude and her excitement and adventurous spirit were very contagious. As far as Kaitlin was concerned, Fred was not amused by the over-exaggerated negative comments and Jo's theatrical antics. They laughed heartily, then the phone rang, breaking up the conversation.

It was Rob. Kaitlin's heart raced with sheer exhilaration, and her stomach filled with butterflies. Such an emotional hold he already had on her, she thought, that it could be fatal, but as his voice came over the phone, detecting a slight nervousness, he apologized for ringing so soon. He wanted to know if she would be interested in going to dinner that night and, in the same sentence, stated that he realized it was short notice. He explained that he wasn't staying long in town, so he thought it would be an excellent time to utilize the opportunity. Secretly being thrilled, Kaitlin tried to hide such a reaction of joy and hoped that she didn't appear to be too enthusiastic, just in case he was put off. "Okay, will 7:00 pm suit you? If so, I shall make the reservation," said he. "Yes, that will be fine," was her easygoing reply. Then realizing her reaction, he felt like they had been having a relationship for years. He was more than happy that Kaitlin accepted at such short notice. After all, secretly, he had been searching for the perfect, most intimate restaurant in town all day.

Kaitlin dressed slowly and ensured that her perfume lingered in everything she wore, hoping just to create a memory in his mind. She picked the most favorite black dress that had such a dramatic impact on most people, being an off-the-shoulder, long-sleeved, body-hugging mini, wearing black seamed stockings and black diamante high heels. As she stood checking herself in the mirror, Jo commented how sexy she looked.

Fred joking said, "Mm, mm, not bad at all," which gave her sexual confidence. At times, it can be fantastic to think that men affect women at times so positively, even if it was only a friend. Any comment like that would make any girl feel like a million dollars. She had at least half an hour to wait. That was the thing with her. It only took Kaitlin about twenty minutes to get ready due to wearing little makeup and never spending any time on the hair. But then the waiting seemed like hours. Worrying, she hoped he wouldn't stand her up. If he did, he'd better have a good reason. If any man ever stood her up, they would never get another chance unless they had a perfect explanation, and even then, it would only be forgiven due to sustaining a grave injury. No one had done that anyway so far in her relationships, but she had seen her friends suffer from various incidences like that, and her being so sexist, Kaitlin wouldn't stand any nonsense.

Rob arrived ten minutes early, thank God. He looked very smartly attired in his trendy suit, smelling of Drake Moi, which stirred Kaitlin's senses. It was a perfume so sensual that he would be assured of a good result, Rob thought especially having one up on her, could be advantageous. He politely handed her a rose, which was almost sweeping Kaitlin off her feet. Its sweet perfume smelt divine, and its apricot petals felt soft too.

Slipping the Rose into a vase, then introducing him to Jo and Fred, who were basically stunned by the almost identical resemblance to the previous boyfriend David, Jo was almost unable to speak momentarily. Maybe Kaitlin hadn't emphasized to Jo and Fred enough about his appearance. They greeted him friendly, almost like a long-lost pal. It was blatantly apparent that Rob was initially well accepted by them. He felt suspicious of their response. However, without delay, the two departed, venturing off to the surprise restaurant. Rob opened the car door for her, commenting how beautiful she looked. Kaitlin reciprocated on his appearance too. This felt too good to be true, but it would be enjoyable if it lasted. He was aglow with radiant health, and the conversation flowed between the two continually as he drove down the road.

Arriving at the restaurant, being quaintly romantic, each table only seated two people, and the place was lit only by candlelight, giving the atmosphere a touch of intimate elegance. So overwhelmed by it all, Kaitlin sat momentarily silent. It was almost as if words had escaped her for the first time in her life. When he spoke, Kaitlin could feel the gentle side of his nature coming through. Sometimes the words he said were not received by her eardrums, being so mesmerized by his presence. This feeling almost felt unnatural, but her mind kept informing her to stay with it. It was as if her logical mind and realism had escaped her. Could this really be happening? Was the question that played over and over in Kaitlin's mind. It's too good to be true. Maybe this was indeed her twin flame. Reassurance was needed on her behalf, and it would be good for her own welfare to keep the true feelings from bursting out through her total honesty, fighting herself to keep it all under wraps and to remain cool and calm but the chemistry was so strong.

They indeed dined well. The octopus served up by silver service was a meal and a half, the flavor exquisite. The atmosphere had become warm and relaxed, induced by the guzzling of Rickadon Wine. Kaitlin due to her nerves had drunk a little too much. So absorbed in the conversation, causing her to be unaware of her physical actions and continuous drinking. When Rob spoke, he looked deep into Kaitlin's eyes as if searching for some sort of answer, for some kind of understanding as to his own spirit. Wondering what the effect had been upon him, it gave one goose-bumps and her curiosity soared.

Almost as if aware of her thoughts, he quickly reached across to grab her hand to reassure her. She had placed her hand upon the table. On doing so, he knocked over the glass of wine. How embarrassing for him. Even though Kaitlin roared with laughter, it broke off the romantic air instantly. He apologized profusely, and his face virtually lit up like a Christmas Tree. The conversation continued along very generally after that. The waiter wasn't impressed, but that was his problem. If he didn't see the funny side of it, the only thing decent left to do in this situation would be to laugh. Kaitlin thinking, it's a sad thing to see in life when people lose their sense of humor. Basically, they may as well give up as humor is always such great medicine as Wally would say.

Definitely having their fill of food and wine, Rob practically sculled a couple of glasses of water, as he had to drive home and certainly didn't want to be picked up by the breathalyzer. He couldn't afford to lose his license or divulge his identity, especially at this crucial moment in his life. Not only that, there were other people's lives at stake, particularly that of his now precious Kaitlin's. They were the last ones to leave the Restaurant, as everything closed so early in such a small country town.

It had been a beautiful meal, and now sitting in the car driving home, the car seemed to be filled with a magical warm atmosphere that emanated from deep within them both. Even though not a great deal of conversation passed between the two, the sexual, highly contented energy secretly overwhelming them with the magnetic attraction for each other. His vibes reaching out to her, then Kaitlin knew he wanted her just as much as she wanted him, aware that it wasn't just a physical allurement. It was his soul, his warmth, looking at each other silently and smiling simultaneously, then staring through the windscreen before them into the darkness, the road lit only by the tangential rays of the full moon.

It seemed a long drive home, and the road was desolate of any other sign of life. Rob savored his thoughts and wanted to blurt out his emotions, feeling so good just to be with her. If only she knew what he had gone through to be with her tonight. If only he could tell her, but it would spoil everything, as he didn't know her well enough to trust her, and because she was such an honest person, he didn't want to destroy the perfect image that he had already created. He had never felt so good around a woman before. He felt a part of her already. Maybe it was that both their barriers were down because they were both slightly inebriated. He hoped she felt as amazing as he did. He slowed down.

He almost didn't want the feeling to end and certainly didn't want the journey to. He realized that dreams could come true. They only had one kilometer to go, hoping Kaitlin just wouldn't jump straight out of the car when they pulled up in the driveway. He finally broke the peaceful atmosphere by politely enquiring if she had enjoyed the evening. She wanted to blurt out that she had been completely swept off her feet and almost did, except her logical mind came to the rescue to maintain a gentle answer of "it was just beautiful. Thank you so much." His face lit up with a glow. Wanting to reach across and touch his beautiful face, being so close to his aura made her feel so good, but she warned herself against being so brash, although usually, Kaitlin didn't find it any bother touching a total stranger. But she knew this was different and felt doing so could imply a very sexual gesture and, therefore, not wanting to spoil a good thing. Deciding to definitely keep her hands to herself. Pulling up into Fred's farmhouse driveway, both were almost feeling disappointed the journey was over and the night was coming to a close.

Apprehensively, Kaitlin asked him in for coffee, unsure if he would take up the offer. He almost jumped out of the car immediately, surprised by his reaction and wondered why she had hesitated. Maybe it was her ego, just afraid of being rejected. Slipping her key into the front door, she heard the rush of footsteps walking quickly down the hall. Jo's cheerful voice rung so clearly and precisely, stating they had the perfect plan to retrieve the magical love potion. She halted sharply on seeing that Kaitlin was accompanied by Rob. Jo was unaware that Kaitlin had entered the house with anybody else.

Jo's hand covered her mouth hastily, and she said, "Uh, oh," and tried to hide and pass off the conversation with great awkwardness. Kaitlin wanted to know straight away, but it was terrible timing having to bide her time to know the idea, unable to divulge any information in front of Rob. Kaitlin was instantly excited and desperate to see the plan. Rob detected this, and there was no way he would get in the way of Kaitlin's wild little spirit. He touched her arm and gently said, "Maybe I had best go. We can catch up on the coffee later." Her heart sunk briefly, feeling like she was torn between the two, but she gently said, "Okay. I'll show you out, Rob," walking back down the hall.

Jo sunk back behind the door and into the kitchen. The old hurricane lamps lit the hallway, making Rob's presence seem so appealing. Kaitlin wanted to just hug him and hold him so close. When he got to the door, he came near to her. Rob gently reached out for her forearm and drew Kaitlin so close to him. He thanked her for such a fantastic night and sincerely told her how beautiful she was. Reaching up to touch his face, his look was so warm, it seemed the natural thing to do. He placed his big hands down on her shoulders and leaned down to kiss her cheek. It was so lovely. Kaitlin looked up at him and couldn't believe she actually felt a little nervous. Rob stated that she didn't need to venture out into the cold just to see him off. He was trembling slightly himself, looking into each other's eyes.

Kaitlin put her arms up around his neck and pulled him toward her, kissing him on the lips. He wanted to break into a tremendous passionate kiss, but they both halted. The air was electric, and Kaitlin was covered in goosebumps. It was a pretty frightening thought, so Kaitlin pulled away and smiled sweetly. Rob said it was time he left with a cheeky grin. He embraced her with the most caring, soft hug. It is truly amazing how much feeling, sincerity, and genuineness can be projected from someone's hug. It's pure physical evidence of how someone actually feels towards you, even though many people aren't aware of it. That's when it's good to realize that you have grown to understand the gift of being assertive and receptive to be able to pick up on the energy so clearly.

They said their goodbyes, all starry-eyed. Rob said he'd call the following day if that was okay, as he didn't want to impinge too much into her life. She explained she really didn't mind, even though tomorrow Kaitlin would be kicking herself, because she would have a hangover, knowing how alcohol affected her body, and realizing the wine they consumed was full of preservatives. Her philosophy of too much of a good thing is terrible for you had definitely gone out of the window tonight, that's for sure, although thinking he really didn't mind that much, as he probably felt the same. He slipped away, driving back into the night.

Shutting the door quickly behind her, she ran back down to the kitchen to investigate the apparent newly concocted plan of attack to retrieve the magical love potion. Fred and Jo had come up with the idea of creating a sizeable accidental fire caused by the magical love potion overheating, a chemical ignition. Fred has seen it on the TV in one of those Australian Police stories of chemical fertilizers etc, and chemicals mixed together overheat and catch on fire. It was so corny though, it could actually work. It was looked upon by Jo and Kaitlin with great humor, but they had to steal back their magical love potion and make it appear that it had overheated, ignited, and blown itself to smithereens, including the bikers' shed. There would be absolutely no traces of anything left if all went according to plan.

"Just for good measure," ensured Fred. Maybe somewhere down the track, they'd have to pay back the bad karma for the disrespect of abusing someone else's shed. But Fred just didn't want it to look like a crime. It was intended to appear to be a natural accident. On explaining this to them, the two were then engrossed and very much for the idea, but on realizing Kaitlin was sitting next to the open window, the cold breeze wafted in. The feeling someone was staring or listening was slightly unnerving Kaitlin, who suddenly closed the window to block out any such thoughts. It felt strange, but it could have been her imagination, or was it truly intuition, or was it Jimmy, the Ghost? Fred really feared for their safety, so it was imperative to plan the job well, ensuring smooth running without there being an inkling of suspicion. It was reassuring to know he cared so much, although Jo and Kaitlin looked at the situation as adventurous and through rose-colored glasses. Fred was a very practical and down-to-earth guy, he knew there could be consequences if they got caught, and those consequences wouldn't be good.

Discussing the plan thoroughly, they organized the night

and date it would happen, needing to buy a certain amount of equipment. Jo and Fred decided to go down to the city the coming week to collect the necessary gear for this minor mis-demeanour to happen. Kaitlin also wanted to let Wally know what was going on and see if he could help them also concoct a decent plan to rescue their magical love potion. Fred was keen to talk to Wally and see if he could also help out some-how even though Fred knew Wally was to old to make a run for it if he had to. Fred thought Wally might be up for it knowing what Wally was like. They all had to work hard and save a bit of cash to make this job happen smoothly, but you have to sacrifice to gain a bit. Even though they were retriev-ing their magical love potion, they were all, almost feeling guilty about being the thieves in the night, but really, they had tried all the correct legal channels, only to find the so-called supposed goodies were involved in these thefts as well. So much for justice. They'd worked so hard on their authentic magical love potion project. It was only fair they rescue it and reap the benefits of their own fruits of labor. It wasn't as if someone was going to end up with grievous bodily harm anyway. Fred would make sure no one came to any harm, not even the bikers themselves.

Eleven

R ob drove back to his newly rental far-met, amazed at how in the blink of an eye, life can appear one way and then drastically change in a heartbeat. Rob would have to work fast now if he was to get out of his present situation. He would have to return to the biker property tomorrow and organize a fire and bomb-proof safe to be installed and hidden somewhere in the biker property shed. The money from the drug crop deal could be stored in the safe in the biker shed. Although very risky, that would appear to be a great spot to hide the bomb-proof safe and for the upcoming incident that may happen very, very appropriate should the biker shed go up in smoke.

The smell of Kaitlin's strong sensual perfume lingered in the car, and his romantic thoughts were back on to her now. How hypnotic her beauty, bewitching personality, feminism, and caring nature was. It was great to have someone honest for a change who actually liked him. It made him feel whole. When she touched him, he felt so wanted. Just to belong and be validated for being himself was so fulfilling. He would call her tomorrow and ask her over for dinner tomorrow night, knowing now she would turn up, plus it would be an excellent opportunity to get to know her more in a relaxed atmosphere.

Rob went to bed contented that he had actually achieved part of his plan. He had been so lucky to have come to this stage so quickly as far as Kaitlin goes. He could see she was a well sought-after woman and turned many a head when she walked into a room or even down the street.

The gods were indeed working in his favor. It had been a great night that had exceed his expectations. Just to be with her was a mystery and how that had come to pass. He felt so good thinking back to what his father always used to say, which seemed so appropriate in this circumstance: "Whatever you vividly imagine, ardently desire, sincerely believe, and enthusiastically act upon must inevitably come to pass," although Rob hadn't realized that with every positive physical action he had made he had actually been manifesting the whole incident to occur somehow.

After a great sleep, Rob rose early in the morning. He stretched out and did a few exercises, then felt sudden nausea in his guts due to the effects of the wine, but it lasted only momentarily. It appeared foggy, pretty cool, and still slightly dark outside as he looked out the window. It was still somewhat unclear for this hour of the morning. Then again, the daylight saving time had just changed over again, so it was to be expected he made a mental note of that as he would have to account for that in his strategic plan. He showered and dressed quickly this time, pulling out his shabby old biker clothes. They suddenly seemed so foreign now when dressed in these clothes, even though only a short time had passed since wearing them. It felt like eons due to being so caught up by the flood of new circumstances within his life. He felt almost reluctant to return to the biker property and to that old way of life and throw himself back into that leader personality that he usually disguised himself behind. However, he had missed Emily and wondered how she was going with her pregnancy and if Brian had settled down, so much more emotionally.

Venturing down to the shed, unlocking the door then, he uncovered his beloved motorbike. He admired it momentarily and felt sad in one way, foreseeing that soon, he would no longer have his precious prize love. But that's life. One day he would maybe have another one, but he would appreciate those following few rides on his motorbike for the moment.

Starting her up, it gurgled and ticked over, like music to his ears. Opening the shed door completely, he then manoeuvred his magnificent machine through the opening of the door. The sun was so slow to rise this morning. He was glad now of his faithful old leather jacket as the bracing wind had a real bite to it as he sped along the dark winding road.

By the time he appeared in the biker property's driveway, the sun had begun to warm the rich red-brown soil. The dew was visible on the luscious green leafy vines, and the country air was so fresh and clean as it hit his nostrils. Dismounting the sensational motorbike, his face ruddy from his cold journey, as he turned to step up onto the verandah of the biker house, he saw Emily standing there, looking pleased to see him. Smiling, Emily inquired as to his trip. Then Rob saw her facial expression as he neared closer to the door. Rob could sense she detected there was something different about him.

He wanted to hug her but decided not to, as it was crucial to treat her as he always had done. She looked healthily aglow.

Rob passed by her without much conversation, as it was best to say nothing. He wanted to tell her something but he couldn't as much as he liked her, because he didn't trust many people. Besides, Rob had work to do and not a great deal of time before returning to his secret farm down the road later that evening. He checked in with the boys and was interested to hear how the drug crop was coming along.

Carlos, as usual, had the most to say and had taken the liberty to pull up all the cannabis plants, which had now seriously headed ready to be sold. He had hung all the cannabis plants upside down from the biker shed ceiling. Now they would have to wait for the formation of the highest concentration of resin to sink down through the leaves. This would make for perfect Dacca. When Rob checked them out, the cannabis plants were looking pretty good. This large guerilla marijuana crop would bring them a great buck or two, he thought. Or should we say him? There was much to do, so he listed his priorities, gave his orders to the guys, then returned to the biker house to make a few phone calls. He rang the Police Officer to organize a meeting for the Police Officer to collect the money of the Top Man. Rob demanded that it would need to be in the next couple of days. He wanted this operation organized before Saturday night, and he wanted the money stored in the secret safe by Friday.

This time there was definitely going to be no stuffing around. If the Top Man wasn't interested in the drug crop or the payoff, Rob would take the deal elsewhere and in the quickest possible manner, no matter what the cost. Although he would ensure that if worst came to worst, one of the other guys would carry the brunt, and Rob's hands would be wiped clean, he didn't feel the need to plan that far ahead, as Rob was always so confident. He knew that the drug deal would run smoothly, as, at the present time, there seemed to be an inevitable shortage of Dacca on the streets. With this much on offer, the Top Man surely wouldn't refuse Rob's deal. Rob was prepared to do a good bargain this time, as he wanted to get the money and get out. Rob realized he had to sacrifice a bit to gain a bit this time. His time was running out. He had contacted the Police Officer over the phone, who had immediately rushed out to see him. It was impossible to speak on the phone, as one never knew who could overhear such a conversation, especially on a country party line. The odd one or two gossiping telephone operators tended to listen in to conversations, who actually thrived on spreading malicious tales of the local townspeople. Where they were concerned, nothing was sacred.

The Police Officer made contact with the Top Man. Then came the wait. This Top Man loved to play out a bit of a power game. Knowing the guy's tactics well, Rob knew he would be inconvenienced and would have to wait at least two hours before the man would be in touch to organize the meeting time and date. Rob grew impatient after four hours, angrily thinking, bugger this guy. He'd go elsewhere with the drug deal. Almost as if aware of Rob's train of thought, the Top Man rang. Rob made sure he let the landline telephone ring for a short duration as he realized who it would be. The Top Man was in agreement as they spoke in a sort of coded dialogue. Inwardly Rob breathed a great sigh of relief. It had been a most productive day. They then had to produce this great crop, all packed and sorted within the next few days. The biker guys would have to induce the process by providing a more heated tropical environment in the shed. This would mean they would have to work hard and fast, Rob would rely on the biker group to do the all-night job. Rob had to return to his little far-met retreat before nightfall. He was on a mission and had to do other tasks to be prepare.

Besides, he still had to call Kaitlin to organize dinner. Christ, what would he cook for her? Maybe he could cheat and visit the health food shop on the way home, grab heaps of healthy cooked food, and just make out he had cooked it. Not such a sincere action, but under the circumstances, he felt he could cook just as well, or so he tried to convince himself. With a slight smirk on his face, he thought it over in his head and justified his actions.

He came into the kitchen and informed Emily that he would not be staying on the biker property for the next few nights but would be around during the day. He used the excuse that he had a great deal of business to attend to if they would get this drug deal wrapped up. If they all wanted to get their cut, then he had to make it work for them. Emily actually believed him, as she had overheard Rob in the conversation with the Top Man on the landline. However, she still had a slight feeling of suspicion somewhere deep inside her. Still, she knew that was her own mistrust issues rearing their head. Rob stealthily mounted his majestic motorbike and skilfully sped off, away from the biker property without a moment to spare.

Twelve

Returning to his new hideaway farm, locking up the motorbike in the obscure rear shed. Hiding any evidence that he may have even been remotely associated with a group of drug dealing bikers. Rob raced in through the door to phone his precious Kaitlin. As her voice came over the line, he relaxed, sinking back into her soft tone of voice, turning back into his own natural personality he knew to be his own.

Rob raced around the small house, cleaning everything up. Plates, groceries, and utensils were strewn in many directions, probably not in some of the most appropriate cupboards, but he doubted whether Kaitlin would be looking into them. Rob hid all the food containers deep in the bin to conceal evidence that he hadn't actually prepared this magnificent vegetarian feast himself. Rob ran the garbage outside down to the bins down the back of the small property. He didn't have time to sort it all into the correct bins for Green Saver. He realized that momentarily he would be contributing to the breakdown in the ozone layer, but at this point in time Rob didn't have time. He hoped there weren't any Greenies around watching him. This small town was very environmental as this was the new thing now in this era.

Rob raced back into the tiny house, almost diving into the shower, hiding his biker clothes in one of the spare wardrobes in the other bedroom. He put on his denim shirt and jeans. Rob checked his gold Datejuss watch, then lit some incense, dimmed the lights, and grabbed candles for the table. Just as he was doing that, a gentle knock on the door startled him, unprepared for her early arrival. Is she always this punctual? He thought.

Revisiting that annihilating thought, at least on the upside, he didn't have to sit around waiting. There was nothing worse than that, feeling that maybe no one would turn up. How distraught does that make one feel, and definitely not good for anyone's ego?

Rob opened the door to Kaitlin, who looked so warm and inviting. Rob stood mystified. "Aren't you going to ask me in?" she said with delightful laughter. He smiled. "Sure, come on in." God, he looked good, she thought, sitting straight down at the table, making herself totally at home. Her stomach cried out in starvation. It appeared that he'd made quite an effort. Which Kaitlin commented on, Rob nodded in happy silence and thought to himself, it's incredible how some things can deceive one without one realizing. Still, the food smelt terrific, especially after coming in from the fresh cool air, hoping like hell it tasted that good. Rob was just as hungry, although he had reassured her that his cooking was good. They chatted about the day. Although he didn't seem to have much to tell of his. He almost brushed it aside with great disinterest as he busied himself in the quaint tiny inviting kitchen. Dinner smelt so good and very wholesome. He served it up, the bowl of lentils being so hot he almost burnt his fingers, restraining from overeating, not wanting to appear to be too much of a glutton. But he seemed to really enjoy his food, though. Nothing like a good healthy appetite. "Are you sure you cooked this and not somebody else?" jokingly inquired Kaitlin. "Do you think I would do something like that," his reply being very misleading by such use of reverse psychology an intelligent move at this point nonetheless and Rob quite often used a technicality to erode reasonable doubt, it had always seemed to work for him over the years.

The warm atmosphere and fullness in their bellies dispelled a relaxation over both of them, almost to the point of them falling asleep, both being so contented with neither feeling a need to be greatly conversant. Rob put on his jumper, as he was feeling the cool chill of the seasonal air change, then he ushered her over to the couch of his small comfortable lounge room, inquiring if she was interested in watching a video. Kaitlin asked what assortment did he have, not much being his answer.

"This one here's pretty horrific. It's on satanism," secretly picking that particular one purposefully, only for the simple reason that Rob remembered what his father had told him as a boy. "If ever you want a girl to get close to you, take her to see a horror movie. She'll grab you and hug you so tight she'll almost rip your shirt off, especially in the scary parts." As that thought passed, Rob laughed to himself.

Kaitlin, quick to detect something suspicious, replied," I cannot stand scary movies, and I'm dead against stuff like that because it's against my metaphysical beliefs. Satanism, in my opinion, only conjures up bad energy and bad karma."

Rob looked at her in total bewilderment at what had just sprouted from her mouth. "Excuse my ignorance," said he softly, "but was that some foreign language you spoke because I don't understand what you just said. What is Karmo?" He realized Kaitlin's equivocalness could be coming at the most inappropriate time and trying to bow out of the conversation gracefully. However, he insisted upon the information, therefore, giving Kaitlin no alternative, even though knowing this could, by his own ignorance, cause him to be put right out of the picture as far as she was concerned. Quickly assessing her thoughts, "It's not Karmo, it's karma, and that is the simple law of metaphysics." "Meta who?" he said. Momentarily, there was a pause, so Kaitlin continuing on, "It actually means in a nutshell, cause and effect, so whatever one physically acts upon, thinks, speaks and feels, affects everybody in their surroundings, the environment, and the world as a whole," said she. "That sounds like pretty heavy shit." Rob had an intent look of concentration on his face. "So, what does that mean?" "Well," replied Kaitlin, "it means all the good things you do come back to you, and so do all the bad, either in this life or the next."

Rob raised his eyes to the ceiling. "Is this true? That's what I would call frightening," he replied. "So, what will happen to me?" "Hey, calm down. It's not all that scary. Once you have been enlightened, you can sort it all out, in a way." "How?" he said inquisitively. "At home, we have so many books on all this stuff. Maybe I could loan them to you, so perhaps you could find your own answers, as it is so in-depth, it can sometimes take a long time to work out what suits you and what you believe for your own soul's journey.

The old grandfather clock struck twelve, startling the two, jolting both back out of such a deep conversation. Kaitlin inquired why it hadn't sounded off before. Rob replied that It only went off at 12:00 pm at night, and he hadn't been able to change it.

"Good Lord. Is it that late? We must have been so engrossed in the conversation that time had slipped away," said Kaitlin. She didn't want to go, but it was time she left. Her rising time in the morning was 5.00 am, and the responsibility of a nurse was so demanding, therefore preferring to avoid the added stress of being tired. As much as her heart wanted to stay, the logical mind knew it was time to leave.

Rob didn't want Kaitlin to go. He almost offered her to stay for the night, but Kaitlin knew there was only one bedroom and one double bed. Rob still felt it wasn't good timing to make that sort of move yet, given her definitely being such a strong character, had her own mind. He wasn't sure if he'd end up with a black eye or not, not wanting to put himself in the situation, avoiding tempting fate. Escorting her to the door, his arm tenderly around her shoulders, she nestled into his body. Opening the door to greet the bitter cold air, walking arm in arm out onto the verandah, down the steps, and to the car, he opened the car door for Kaitlin, who apologized for leaving so hurriedly. He understood the need for responsibility. He admired her for her attitude, thinking to himself how he really did like a lot of her traits,

Thanking him for the lovely evening, the brisk air stung their cheeks, contemplating her departure. He drew her close and kissed her so passionately. He felt her melt into his arms. Her body writhed into him to become warm. Her hand ran up and down his back underneath his jumper. Even though it wasn't directly on his skin, he could still feel how cold her hands were. He sighed. "Your hands are freezing."

Quick with the comment of "cold hands warm heart," Kaitlin laughed. He smiled and said, "Hey, I bet," and kissed her again, tearing himself away and suggesting strongly and caring it was a good idea to get in the car as she might catch a cold. She agreed, got in, wound down the window, and stated that he was welcome over to Fred's farmhouse tomorrow night. Therefore that would give him a chance to get to know Fred and Jo, have some dinner, and check out some of the books that they'd been discussing. He accepted the offer and inquired as to a suitable time. The arrangements were made, and she drove off. He slowly walked back inside feeling good, aware that his whole life had begun to change to be so much better.

To a certain degree, it was too late to stop the tidal wave of change now. Rob didn't want to anyway. He felt in some way that he wasn't holding the reigns in this entire situation. This was an unnerving tangibility, this being the first time his heart had ever ruled his head. He was attempting to come to terms with this emotion which was the hard part, and not to get hurt was an alarming cerebration. Rob knew that Kaitlin felt the same way he did. Although nothing had been said, he also knew that he had been deceitful, playing on her vulnerability in a certain way. Realizing that as far as his appearance went, his being identical to David, the dead boyfriend, maybe could be a big part of the initial attraction Kaitlin had to him.

He hoped that Kaitlin really liked him for his own personality, although after their discussion tonight, he really wasn't sure if he was worth being liked. The guilt churned in his guts, thinking about everything he had gone through just to meet this woman, but it had been with good intent. Still, in a state of shock regarding this karma business, he'd never heard of it before. This higher mental awareness she talked of. He'd seen a few books on the power of the mind at some stage in his lifetime but never had a need to read such books, already knowing he was brilliant, whereas he had always thought there was only one intelligence now, not sure if that was right. Realizing he was learning a lot, but it was totally a different way of thinking than he had ever encountered. Curious as to how many other people thought like it, wondering why he had never experienced such information before, and fully aware that Kaitlin was highly intelligent in her own right.

That night he had been bombarded by so many thoughts from his mind. With this new awakening into his conscious mind, he found it incredibly difficult to sleep, tossing and turning, his mind tormented by the turmoil. The anguish caused his brain to speed up, feeling now as though it was accelerating at a hundred miles per hour. Drifting in and out of the light realms of sleep. He began to break into a sweat, his mind reflected back into the past. Incidences flashed past, causing him to realize that hiding behind the biker image was not good armor. It had been such a false facade.

Aware of an apparition standing next to the bed. The ghost was dressed in Rob's biker clothes, although the figure, standing there ghost-like and in a haze, its voice being of an obviously different tone altogether, forewarning him vigilantly, "Don't you dare hurt my Kaitlin. She feels very strongly toward you. If you cause her any harm, I shall harm you, as I am of the spirit world, the unknown. You are only in the physical now. You are unaware of my power. Against me, as a man, you will be helpless. You, Rob, are at a crossroads. You already know how you feel about Kaitlin. All I ask is that you be honest with her, even if you decide this relationship is not for you. Be honest with her, Just remember. Just what Jimmy has said to you, You set the spell of, it's all your own doing, and now I am here, remember, you just remember. Jimmy faded into the shadows.

Rob felt a deathly cold hand touch his bare chest where his heart was centered. Suddenly aware it was so real, a severe nervousness rushed through his body. A panic attack overtook him. Screaming from the depths of his stomach, terrified and suddenly wide awake, jumping out of bed aggressively, he turned on the light. Questioning himself, was he dreaming? Had he seen a ghost? What was the time? The clock's face revealed the numerals at 4:30 am. His hands trembling he walked out of the bedroom, turned on the passage light, stepping into the kitchen, he poured himself a glass of milk, aware he was saturated in perspiration, leaving the hall light on, hating to admit to the fear. How could this woman have such an effect on his life? Then switching on the television, turning it down to a soft monotone, trying to soothe his nerves, wishing she was there to hug and comfort him.

What was happening to his mind? The whole situation occurred when he really needed to be together to be mentally alert and in control. He didn't envisage that leaving his heart so open would lead to an internal conflict in his head. Things happen in life when they are least expected. That's life, sometimes as much as we don't want to know about it. Having absolutely no intention of breaking away from Kaitlin, especially at this point in time, he'd worked too hard and sacrificed too much just to meet her. He drifted eventually off into a disturbing light sleep.

The alarm sounded like a siren echoing loudly in his eardrums. Rob woke with a start. On waking, he realized he was mentally drained and wanted to sleep at least another eight hours, but knowing the pressure was really on to get organized today. For starters, a heavy day lay ahead, having to get back to the biker property and check on how the drying process for the cannabis was progressing. He was also in the throes of finalizing the meeting with the Mafia Assailant, before finally arriving back at the biker property. Rob was feeling totally exhausted already.

On entering the biker house, it held an unusual air of cessation for 7:30 am. in the morning. Entering the bedroom to collect his diary, requiring numerous telephone numbers from it to make the various calls, on walking in, he passed the lounge room overcome with the stench of bong water. They're visible on the coffee table was a bong tipped over on its side, lying in a pool of grotty stinking water. Dope, matches, and ashtray lay strewn about on the tabletop. The room reeked of the smell of cannabis. His temper rose from within, rushing outside to check the large back shed.

Rob instantly concluded that, obviously, Carlos was making his own underhanded plans in the drug deal. If he was, he would pay dearly. The biker shed was stacked with hundreds of plastic bags full of dope, all packed up neatly. The bikers must have toiled for hours through the night to complete such an amount of work. The drugs had all been weighed and sorted appropriately. Rob was appalled by Carlos's deceitfulness even though knowing all along the man was a ruthless excuse of a human being who could never be trusted. He raced back to the biker house, this time passing through the kitchen where Emily peacefully sat in her favorite chair, with coffee in hand, disrupted by Rob's sudden burst into her tranquility, looking up from her magazine. Rob's stern voice fired such direct questions at her, unable to lie to him and wouldn't under the circumstances, knowing that he definitely wasn't in the mood to be messed around. Emily felt Rob looked so tired and was so grumpy anyway.

Explaining that Carlos and a few of the guys had been bonging on the last few nights after Rob left the biker property. Emily continued to explain. Carlos, of course, was the ringleader, which confirmed in Rob's mind his own gut feeling, Rob never voicing an opinion to Emily. Emily was glad to get it off her chest, feeling a great loyalty in some respects to Rob and an intense disliking to Carlos. Rob knew that Emily and Brian hadn't been involved in any ruthless back dooring behavior. He knew they didn't smoke dope, especially since Emily became a pregnant health fanatic. Her eyes held no trace of the after-effects of THC, that's for sure. Rob's temper brewed within like a volcano awaiting eruption.

Carlos then staggered blurry-eyed into the kitchen. "Hey, Em." He laughed, still slightly stoned. "What's happening, man?" Unfortunately, he didn't see Rob standing behind the door. Emily rose quickly from the table. Feeling it was time to vacate the room due to the tension she saw rising. She preferred to keep right out of this one with Carlos and Rob.. Brian was moving around under the clothesline outside starting to hang out all the washing, Emily darted outside to the laundry to check on the washing and joined Brian under the clothesline who put his arm around her comfortingly, gave her a peck on the check and they happily hung out all the clothes.

Carlos stood, aimlessly staring out of the window at the two, jealous as all hell, still unaware that Rob was behind and standing there staring at him. As soon as Emily vacated the room, Rob moved quickly and precisely, stalking his prey. Then Carlos, stirred by the sudden noise behind, turned swiftly. His movements are too slow to counteract Rob's. Carlos was pinned to the wall instantly by Rob's body, and his large, strong hands tightened firmly around Carlos's throat. Rob's calm deep clear voice penetrated Carlos's ears. What's your story, dog?"

Carlos, almost stuttering, unable to hide his fear, "What, Do ya mean, boss?" "You know exactly what I mean. One person you should never stuff around with, Carlos, is me," stated Rob. At this stage, Carlos's face becoming cyanosed and his body perspiring from nerves. "Sure, sure, boss," he agreed as Rob pushed him into the wall again. "Okay," repeated Carlos. "Now get the hell out to the shed, pack all that dope into those boxes, and load up the god damn truck. I'm getting rid of all these drugs today. You can all have your money and get out of here."

Rob rang the Top Man. They organized a time to meet

and do the drug deal at the cross-bridge for 2:00 pm. It was now 8:30 am. Rob ordered the guys to do the work, as he was exhausted. Rob supervised as the guys pitched in to pack every last bit of dope into the small van. Rob decided they were going to the venue at least a couple of hours earlier to case the joint out and make sure it wasn't a set-up. One could never be too careful, thought Rob, especially dealing with people like this.

Rob decided to follow the small van on his motorbike. Rob had never exposed himself physically to the Top Man but had only had dealings with the guy over a landline phone and phone box and through other sources. Although curious to meet this guy, he refrained on this occasion, thinking perhaps some other time. Carlos was now told to park the van off the road on the other side of the cross-bridge. That's the side the Top Man would be parking on. Carlos had ordered that he and Rolf would meet with a black limo, count the money, ensuring there was a million dollars cash in the brief-case. Then Carlos and Rolf would walk back on the left side of the road as close to the bridge railing as possible. Rolf was to walk right next to the barrier. He was pulled aside by Rob, who informed him secretly if anything happened, grab the case from Carlos and throw it over the side of the bridge. In the area, rains had been so severe of late, the flooded creeks were all running into the Murray River. The Murray River water was sweeping through in volumes quite fast underneath the bridge. However, it wasn't up to the spoon drain level yet, which was covered over by four-foot small steel cage doors, adding extra strength and safety for the general public.

Using his pencil torch, Rob surveyed inside the large

man-sized drain outlet and shone the torch through the iron grate covering it. Out of curiosity, he tried to wedge it open it came ajar very slightly, and then he closed it snap very quickly. The large tunnel through the middle of the bridge led inwardly for about 30 meters to another outlet, which came out facing into a great deal of vegetation and a group of large white gum trees. Here Rob could camouflage his motorbike, which would be way out of sight, and he could remain undetected but present, observing clearly the drug deal about to take place. This spot would be inconspicuous and easily accessible to the main road back to the biker property should he have to make a quick getaway undetected. Not that Rob was planning anything along those lines as yet. Walking back through the sizeable cylindrical cement tunnel, he could watch from underneath the bridge to ensure Carlos did the right thing by Rob and the other bikers. Rob checked his old biker watch. Rob ensured all the five other bikers were organized in their perspective places way out of sight. Carlos and Rolf sat patiently in the parked van on the side of the road.

Rob situated himself underneath the bridge, well out of sight, although he had excellent visibility. He organized the small biker group half an hour early as he wasn't taking any risks, hoping the event would run smoothly and soon be over, so Rob could finally get some rest. Rob crouched down and pulled out some cheese sandwiches from the backpack Emily had made for this trip. Not the most lavish lunch, but nonetheless, better than nothing, especially when he was starving.

Emily really was a gem, he thought, admiring the breathtaking, peaceful scene and listening to the rushing sound of the water as it cascaded past where he stood. Almost on the last bite of his sandwich, he looked up ahead. Winding down the road from a distance appeared to be a Police Patrol car. Taken aback for a second. Rob was left no time to alert the guys without revealing his presence. The Police Patrol car stopped on the opposite side of the cross-bridge at the opposite end to the van. This is odd, was the thought passed through Rob's mind, who was frowning as he hadn't been informed the Police Officer would be here. A voice wailed to Carlos. Not to worry, thought Rob. It was only that sludge and local Police Officer, as Rob thought, that he has probably turned up for his cut of the money. Rob underneath the cross-bridge heard another car engine halt on the other side of the cross-bridge, moving unobserved very cautiously to one side to spy and keep a check on Carlos.

Two suited up Mafia men appeared from the big black limo. They opened the back of the Van, checked out the stock, sniffing some of the bags. Then Carlos and Rolf were ordered to walk toward the limo. The electric window came down, the word was given, and a large black leather briefcase was handed out. Carlos opened it. His eyes sparkled with greed. He put his hand in to touch it, making it blatantly apparent that he had never seen so much money before, closing it up quickly, guessing that Rob would possibly be watching.

Both Carlos and Rolf proceeded to walk back toward the van, just as Rob had advised them to, both nervously turning when the small van engine started up and drove off in the opposite direction. The limo remained there humming momentarily. As they neared the halfway mark on the cross-bridge. Almost close to the vicinity where Rob was situated down below. He remained well out of sight but observed their every move vehemently. Carlos could hear the slow creeping limo proceeding behind them, speaking anxiously to his biker assailant, "We're being followed. Let's hurry. Let's walk faster."

The car began to speed up slightly but was still situated a fair distance behind them. Swiftly Rolf grabbed the briefcase from Carlos. Instantaneously both ran for their lives, filled with fear, suddenly two gunshots rang across the wide-open expanse of the road, hitting and knocking Carlos immediately to the ground, then again another, this time at the other biker Rolf, who was shot in the shoulder. He staggered like a wounded dog over to the railing. Another bullet hit him, only just managing to get up enough strength to throw the briefcase over the side. It hit the ground. Rob raced out from under the cement cross bridge and grabbed the briefcase. Aware of what was happening, he could hear both cars from either end driving fiercely to meet in the middle of the bridge just above him. Rob quickly emptied all the money into his knapsack. He couldn't get it all in. Two of the wads had come loose in the briefcase. He promptly threw the briefcase along with the loose money out into the raging current of water and darted back undetected under the cross-bridge hidden from view and well out of sight. The briefcase, however, could be clearly seen by all being briskly whisked away by the surging current along with many loose notes swiftly downriver. Hearing an avalanche of yelling voices and aware the people were directly above him, acting in a disorderly and verbally uncontrollable fashion, he hurried back to the cage door of the spoon drain. Quietly slipping through without disturbing the ground around the entrance. Once safely inside, he closed the cast iron gate securely behind him, appreciating his intuition and the fact that he had perceived such a plan of action as a backup. Immediately running like an athlete farther down the tunnel of the drain, suddenly stopping steadfast in his tracks for one second, his heart racing and entirely breathless, he was so tired the day had felt like a lifetime, and it was only mid-afternoon. What now was to be his course of action? Certainly not counting on these events taking place.

Now having actually been a witness to two murders, he would bury it deep in his consciousness for the moment and he knew he would have to deal with it at a later date. Man, it wasn't his fault. Lucky enough to decline to take on the job himself today, his mind raced, having to get back to the biker property. That way, he would be safe. Hearing the engines of the cars above him drive off hastily, running then to the end of the tunnel almost as fast as a speeding bullet, then he checked first for safety, then emerged through the outlet. Way off in the distance, he could see with his binoculars the big Police Officer chasing along the riverbank, with the Top Man trying desperately to catch the briefcase and all the money floating in the water. Just when the Top Man attempted to fish out the case, it submerged itself quickly, straight down the deep drainage system, which stretched for miles underground and emptied out into the sea. Unfortunately for the crooks, they lost the briefcase forever. Serve's the bastards right, thought Rob. All parties had all left the main road and the homicide scene very quickly.

Rob mounted his motorbike, clearing his path briskly, taking off without even leaving a trace of his presence behind as he drove over the cross-bridge. He dared not even look at his dead counterparts lying slumped on the side of the road, almost out of eye-shot. Rob sped hastily back to the biker property. When he'd hidden the money safely in the biker shed, quickly assembling the remaining bikers together to explain the situation, some were quite shocked and hadn't thought that the situation would get this far out of hand, but when you play with fire, you're bound to get burnt. Rob paid them all a couple of thousand dollars each. That was enough for them at present to keep their mouths shut and split from the biker property immediately. Many of the bikers packed and left in a flash without question knowing that the money had gone downstream in the heist.

Emily was most upset about the deaths and preferred not to know anything. Just as the old saying goes, the less you know, the better off one is, so she opted out halfway through the conversation. Rob could understand. She was easily excused. He didn't really want to upset her in her present condition, not really knowing how to deliver a baby or needing the responsibility right now as the baby was closer to being due.

Rob felt too tired to derive a plan but knew he must solve his present situation, foreseeing that within a short time, he would hear from the Top Man or the Police Officer in regards to the matter at hand. Fast organization was required in his mind, and Rob plotted the alibi. When the phone rang half an hour later, it was the Top Man, and Rob was surprised that now he had resolved another problem and the Top Man was in debt to him. Rob secretly provided Emily and her boyfriend with thousands of dollars. The topic was dismissed and never discussed again.

Well in the clear, Rob now mounted his motor bike, bade Emily and Brian goodbye, and drove back to his hideaway retreat. Once there, he locked up his bike in the rear shed, raced in, peeled off his clothes, and sat in the bottom of the shower, leaving the hot water to run soothingly over his toned spent body. If Rob was ever really contemplating writing a novel, at least it would be a best seller. With the information he would divulge in it, probably questioning a few of the characters involved in the well-talked about controversial drug inquiry going on in Australia at the present moment, which reminded him that he had better write something on his note pad.

Kaitlin had already quizzed him on it, actually catching him off guard. Rob didn't want her to think that he hadn't come here to actually write a novel. Out of the shower, dressing quickly, unable to remember what time Rob was due at Kaitlin's, deciding to go early. He really needed to see her. She was so uncomplicated in her own sweet way, and he needed the affection, especially after such a traumatic day. Tonight definitely, he would be back here, home early to give himself the chance to get some sleep.

Thirteen

Driving hastily to Fred's farm, arriving as she was just about to head off for a jog. She looked great in her singlet and striped lycra running shorts. What a body. Rob hadn't seen so much of her revealed until this time. "Are you joining me?" said she. "I wasn't expecting you so early." He stepped from the car. Kaitlin felt there was something wrong. He looked like a wreck. Walking toward her, she put her arms around him and cuddled into him. He was so glad to see her. It was as though the rest of the world had now disappeared. "Why don't you come for a run? It might make you feel better." He replied, "How do you know how I'm feeling?" She laughed it off. "Well, I'm psychic, you know." She laughed.

Thinking quietly, thank God she wasn't that psychic, he jest-fully, sarcastically replied, "Oh, that's right. I forgot." He laughed. It was good to laugh. Great medicine after such an ordeal today. Deep down, Kaitlin knew there was something seriously wrong but didn't press the issue. Kaitlin ran back into the house, organized a singlet, some cycle nicks, and sandshoes of Fred's for him to wear. Off down the road went the two. Honestly, Rob was so stuffed. What a madcap idea, he thought. Love definitely made him act strange. He was sure he'd never really done something like this for any other woman, especially while being so physically exhausted.

She laughed and joked as she ran ahead of him. She had bounds of vitality to match her vivacious personality. He tried desperately to keep up, but his pace slowed to a shuffle. He was breathless. Man, how fit was, Kaitlin. Kaitlin turned to seek his whereabouts. He was lagging well behind. Feeling slightly guilty for dragging him out on the course when Rob had looked so bad at the start, she turned around, and they headed back off home. He sprawled on the verandah, totally stuffed. Kaitlin, perspiring, sitting down next to him, leaned down to kiss him on the cheek. Feeling such an impulsive sexual attraction to his body, tapping him on the chest. "Come on. Let's go have a shower. Jo's got the tea cooking. You can have your shower first and don't be long."

All four sat chatting at the kitchen table, becoming heavily involved in a conversation about the ozone layer and environmental issues. The atmosphere was pleasant, although now it was 8:30 pm. Jo and Fred excused themselves and bade them goodnight, explaining that they had to be up at the crack of dawn.

Now both were alone in front of the open fire. "By the way, these are those books I was telling you about last night." She pointed to the bookshelf where dozens of books lined the bookshelf. Just take anyone you feel is appropriate for you."

He just grabbed a couple without really thinking about it. He lay on the floor, fighting with his eyes to stay open. He knew he had to drive quite a distance back to his hideout. He explained to Kaitlin what had happened to him the previous night with his dream. She had a greatly concerned look on her face. She looked so beautiful in the dimly lit room.

"I feel perhaps you need to go home and get a good night's sleep," gently stroking his face and running her fingers through his hair. "Maybe we'd better not see each other to-morrow night." His heart sank, but he understood and agreed even though he would miss seeing her. He quickly kissed her goodnight, and they parted. She hoped he could stay awake long enough to make it safely home. He crashed on the bed, fully clothed, instantly falling into a profound sleep.

The following morning he didn't hurry back to the biker property as now the mission there had been accomplished. The last couple of bikers had been paid by Rob, who were currently waiting for the celebrations at the shindig Saturday night. They were also waiting for the end of the week to come to collect their regular dole checks and be paid their cash wages from the grapevine owners. Then they would be skipping out of town! Heading back to the city. It had been a while since Rob had done any work on his bike. That seemed his sole purpose today. Rob hadn't told the others the exact amount of money he had rescued, so tonight, he would take three-quarters of a million with him that no one else knew he had and store it at his hideaway. The bikers had all thought most of the money had gone down the Murray River, and they were happy to receive the substantial sum of cash that Rob had kindly given them with no questions asked.

He made Emily a coffee, and they talked for a while. Brian wandered in quietly checking on Emily and grabbed a spanner out of the kitchen cupboard, silently smiling at Emily then left to go back outside to fix the rainwater tap.

Emily was actually surprised to see this side of Robs nature, never realizing he was or could be so maternal. She discussed hers and Brian's' future plans with Rob. He seemed pleased that she and Brian were happy, had sorted out their lives and differences, and were now having a more solid relationship. "At least you have a chance to kick up your heels on Saturday night at the show," she said to Rob. Rob stated he wouldn't be going, as someone had to stay and look after the biker's property. He knew everybody else was looking forward to Saturday's show. It didn't particularly worry him if he stayed home. "That's a shame," replied Emily, who had never seen these new sides to his character before, and her suspicious mind regarded those thoughts.

Fourteen

Rob stayed on the biker property for tea. He loved Emily's homemade lasagne. It had been a good day for him to mentally relax. He would venture back to this own secret hideaway later and get stuck into reading some of those books that Kaitlin had lent him, and at least maybe conjure up a small understanding of what the true essence of mysticism was about

It had grown very dark, very quickly. The heavy rain began to pelt down on the tin roof. Rob was tempted to stay on the biker property. More so now that he'd even spring-cleaned his room, and it looked so cozy. Donning his leather jacket to keep dry. Rob secretly filled his knapsack with most of the money from the biker shed safe. Leaving some behind, ensuring to lock everything behind him, concealing any evidence, Emily and Brian unsuspecting jubilantly stood together, waving goodbye to him on the verandah. It would be a hazardous journey for him under these weather conditions, wherever he was going, and Emily wondered where that was, especially now that the drug deal was done. Brian explained to Emily that they still weren't out of the woods here. The crooked local Police Officer could come and cause problems for them anytime, so they still had to be on guard.

Rob was away, whizzing past the local town, then approaching Kaitlin's house. In his thoughts, he missed her already. Such a deep love for her had developed over only such a short time. It seemed many events had taken place, almost like a lifetime in a few short weeks. Even his whole attitude about life, himself, and others he had begun to question. Not having had any time to analyze any of it.

Tonight would be an opportunity to sit and ponder, thinking back to her profound words last night, recollecting: "To analyze is to separate out the entangled threads of one's inner life. The analysis must always serve synthesis to serve life. What is taken apart must be put back together again." An exciting concept thought Rob she should have joined the police force.

The road was covered by a great deal of water from the sudden heavy downpour of rain. Rob found it very difficult to hold the bike up on the winding road. Visibility now abysmal by the falling hailstones. As he drove past Kaitlin's, he glanced quickly at the cottage settled back against the moon, then was hit by the sudden emergence of an array of bright solid lights from a vehicle driving on the wrong side of the road. He hastily swerved to miss the four-wheel drive but lost control of his bike, driving straight off the side of the road into the mud, the motorbike hitting the ground and causing the motor to cease, Rob, landing slightly away from his bike on his side in the gravel. Temporarily lying motionless, trying to stand up, the incredible pain shot straight down his leg. The muscles felt dead as if some foreign body had wedged itself into the bone. That bastard driving the four-wheel-drive hadn't even bothered to stop. For all he knew, Rob thought to himself, he could be dead. So much for reporting it. Rob hadn't even been able to distinguish the car's rego number in the dark of the night in the heavy storm.

Limping around in the dark, his knapsack having been so full had actually protected his back, for which he was genuinely grateful. His leg was now excruciating with the pain. With his hand, now feeling down the side of his quad muscle, his jeans appeared ripped, and there was actually a jagged stick lodged deep into the muscle, painful as it would be, it had to be removed. Taking an intense breath, pulling the stick away, quickly leaving behind a trail of blood running down his leg. Although now he could move his leg up slightly, immediate help was required. He was worried. As much as neither he nor Kaitlin were bargaining on seeing each other tonight, bad luck, he was desperate for help, knowing under the circumstances, she wouldn't object.

Limping back up the road about fifteen meters, he rested on the huge exposed rock, the gateway to Fred's farmhouse where Kaitlin lived. Of all nights, it had to be absolutely pissing down with rain, his beautiful motorbike totally wrecked, and him dressed in biker clothes. Just great, this must be what Kaitlin called Karma. "Shit," he yelled, kicking the rock with his other foot, then regretting it, stubbing his toe. What could Rob do? He would have to come clean. She would probably throw him out. They could always elope with all this money he had in his bag. Consumed by his thoughts from such stupidity, he decided to take it as it came as if she'd be that stupid that Kaitlin would elope. He assumed she would definitely be too level-headed for that anyway.

He hobbled, totally frustrated and helplessly down the half a kilometre muddy path that led to Fred's farmhouse. Drenched and in terrible pain, it felt like he had endured miles to get to the front door. Then finally arriving, he stopped to think momentarily of the next course of action. Rob looked to the right of Fred's farmhouse then hobbled over to the clothes line. Pinching Fred's shirt, he removed his own tee shirt and jacket. Putting on the saturated white Guirel shirt, then awkwardly as discreetly as possible, moving to the other side of the farmhouse, slipping his keys into his jeans' pocket, then hiding his jacket, tee-shirt, and knapsack up underneath the base of the tank stand. As he knelt on his wounded leg. The severe pain shot through it, taking his breath away, disinterested to check again, ensuring if it was out of sight, hoping there wasn't any blood, on the impulsively "borrowed" shirt, finally and with great guilt he manoeuvred himself slowly up the stairs of the verandah. Man, his leg hurt, but he felt worse that he was deceiving Kaitlin, wanting to just blurt the whole story out, feeling so vulnerable due to his present situation and the immense physical pain.

He knew it was important to get himself together, banging loudly on the door, knocking continuously and loudly until someone finally came to the door. A startled but sweet little voice, called out "Who is it?" "It's me, Rob. It's Rob. Open the door, please. Please let me in." The door flew back. He was so surprised as she, standing there in her knee-length pink satin singlet night attire, looking totally seductive. She was flabbergasted by his condition. "Christ, what happened to you? Come in. Quick, down to the bathroom. Can you manage? Here, let me help you."

He was saturated, covered in mud and slush, trying not to lean on her as she looked so clean, putting a chair into the sizeable old bathroom and helping him off with his shirt. "What happened, Rob? Do you want to tell me about it? Fred's got a shirt just like this one. You must have the same taste," she said with a smile as she tossed it in the bath to soak. He blushed slightly, then felt like a real bastard, looking the other way to hide his shame. Kaitlin, then observing his blood loss dripping profusely on the floor, instantly investigated its origin. "God, look at your leg. Quick, off with your jeans." "What?" said Rob, with a tremendous indignant tone in his voice. Kaitlin read his resistance. "Well, if you want help, they have to come off, and the sooner, the better because there's obviously a lot of damage under there. Then lovingly reassuringly him, "Hey, Robby. I've seen it all before. Remember, I'm a Nurse. Seen one, you've seen 'em all."

He started to relax, then still with some resistance, carried out her order, removing the jeans slowly, as moving the leg was excruciating but not as bad as before. Kaitlin helped him with the jeans. He stared at her beautiful face. Intensely concentrating on his large leg wound, and at first sight, observing her frown. He was worried. She did her best to reassure him.

"Okay, hop under the shower," being the following order, "I'll get all the gear ready. We will sit near the fire and remove the large splinters out of your leg. It's going to take time." Rob showered briefly, washing away all the mud and slime off of his body. With only a towel around him. Hobbling into the lounge. Kaitlin had set up her antiseptic, tweezers, bandages, sterile dressing tray, and whatever else she would use to attend to his large wound and hopefully be able to fix up his leg and then get him to a Doctor.

"The bleeding has stopped quite a bit, but we need to remove these splinters," said she. Rob sat upright on the large sheepskin rug next to the fire. She moved his towel a little to the side, revealing the wound. What a situation to be in, he thought.

She looked at his face and kissed him on the lips, quickly reassuring him. "You okay?" He nodded his head. She cast her eyes downward toward the wound but also taking in the sight of his washboard abdominal muscles. She was incredibly physically attracted to him, even if it wasn't the most appropriate time. Gently removing all the splinters from his wound, while he looked away, unable to watch, she, being as careful as could be, then packed the wound with a compress of Bitters and Colloidal Silver, an excellent ancient old rapid healing remedy. She turned off the bright light. Now the worst was over. Clearing up most of the so-called tools of the trade, he watched her toiling away with such love in his eyes. She knelt next to his leg. Leaning over, he could see her rounded, firm breast slightly exposed by her low-cut night attire. Unaware of him staring at her, she slowly wrapped and dressed his leg wound. She oozed sex appeal, and knowing she had absolutely nothing under that satin nightie, he was excited by the mere fact. He had to cross his legs slightly, so she wouldn't notice how hard and aroused he had become. Finishing the dressing, she looked at him, saying, "Now would you like a drink of something? Actually, we've got some mild painkillers in the medicine cupboard if you want some. It would probably help till we got you to a doctor."

Rob, instantly on guard, snapped, "No way am I going to a doctor." Kaitlin said, slightly taken aback, "Calm down. It's okay. I'll get those pills for you. Yes, you'll be going because you could end up septic, and I am not going to be responsible for that."

He stared into the fire, sorry and annoyed with himself by his fiery reaction. Kaitlin knelt on the other side of him, offered the two mild painkillers and an elegant stemmed wine glass filled with pure rainwater.

Swallowing them down, he felt heaps better already. His hand now rested on Kaitlin's bare shoulder. "I didn't mean to snap at you, Kaitlin. I'm sorry." She accepted and reassured him that it didn't really matter under the circumstances.

He pulled her gently but so close to his bare chest and kissed her. The passion between them became so intense. She pressed him down into the sheepskin rug. He pulled her body tightly into him. Kissing each other so passionately, he turned toward her, almost lying on his side, taking care not to injure his already wounded leg, which did make things slightly awkward. Her hands ran up and down his spine. He felt incredibly horny, and she felt him pressed so close to her crotch, his hand touching her on her upper thigh, gliding up and down her smooth, silky skin. Then thinking, any minute she might stop him, but she reciprocated by gently running her fingertips over his hip. His hand then followed the contours of her body up under the satin singlet, gently touching and caressing her breast and her nipple, knowing she was just as sexually aroused as he. His heart pounded. He wanted her so much. He wanted to make love to her with such intense passion. Her hand sensuously glided underneath his towel, gently squeezing a muscle in his buttocks. A thought embarked upon him, suddenly said, "What if Jo and Fred come home?" "Don't worry, they're away. They went to stay with Wally," she replied, both giggling. Then he kissed her again, his hand on her behind, pulling her into his groin, lust oozed radiantly between them. He placed her toned leg over his hip, just above his wound, their genitals grinding rhythmically in succession, as they embraced, touched, and aroused each other. He moved his lower half away slightly, moving his hand down gently between her legs, feeling how wet and turned on she was. She undid his towel, and he knew then he had her permission to continue this provocative sexual act. Finding his penis rock hard, she touched it then, sliding her fingers up and down his groin and across his hips, sending sparks of excitement up his spine. He pulled up her satin nightie and rolled her onto her back on the rug. The fire had almost died down, and the room was now dimly lit, even though still warm, the contours of her body, now fully exposed by the dim firelight.

He knelt on his good leg, directly over her naked body. Breaking away from her lips, he kissed her face, stroking her curly long burgundy hair with one hand, his hot tongue, then licking the side of her throat. Moving down over to her right nipple, then her left, he sucked and fondled her breast. She ran her nails up and down his back, around his buttocks, beginning to sigh and moan. Her eyes closed, and enjoying the pleasure of the eroticism. His tongue proceeded in a straight line down her midriff. Passing over, he moved down to the warm wetness between her legs, his hands now stroking her lower abdomen as he playfully licked her clitoris. He was finding it challenging to wait anymore. She, was also impatient with her erotic groaning of excitation, she pulled him up to her, gliding his hard penis between her open legs, teasing her, rubbing his excited penis up and down her clitoris. He became more aroused by the sound of their sexual wetness mixing as their bodies grind-ed together provocatively.

Neither could wait any longer. Gently gliding his hand sensuously into her wet, tight vagina, it felt like heaven to be inside her, his woman. He was afraid he would come straight away. She was an incredible lover and seemed to enjoy every minute of him being inside her and pleasing him more so than any other woman. Almost on the brink of coming, both thrusting sensually together. He moved energetically in and out of her, penetrating deep into her wetness. He could feel her begin to orgasm. Unable to control himself, he ejaculated his semen into her as they came together, both groaning loudly, being united in such an explosion of eroticism. The slithering of their bodies gently died down as he lay on top of her. Kissing each other again and again on the lips, moving down slightly, he lay his head on her breast, listening to her heartbeat, his penis still in her and not wanting to move, both somewhat breathless but feeling totally fulfilled. It really had been worth waiting for, going through such an ordeal for all this to happen, and this was only the beginning, thought Rob to himself. God, he loved this woman. That night he stayed at Fred's farmhouse with Kaitlin, slept in amongst the purple satin sheets of her bed, and made love to her beautiful body another couple of times during the night before his leg became awkward and painful. He felt so in love with her, and she secretly with him, although he couldn't help but tell her he cared so deeply for her and was so relieved to know the feeling was mutual. He jokingly said to her before drifting off into the afterglow, "I can't believe it took an accident for this to happen." Kaitlin's wise reply being, "Sometimes our greatest problem can be our richest opportunity." He had to agree with that one, that's for sure. She really was an amazing woman, he thought to himself. He was so glad that the adventurous Kaitlin was actually in his life.

Fifteen

The following day Kaitlin dressed Rob's wounded leg again, then drove him down to rescue his motorbike, although having to bend the truth a little. Explaining that being a bike mechanic years ago, one of the locals had asked him to fix the bike, and last night while taking it for a test drive, the accident occurred. She didn't question the story much. Checking the damage to the motorbike, he was able to eventually get it started. The two lovingly parted, his leg still aching, but hopefully, it would heal quickly. He reassured Kaitlin he would go to the Doctor. Promising he would as he didn't want to risk losing his leg at this time in his life. Riding the motorbike cautiously and very slowly back to his hideout.

Being Friday and still relatively early in the morning, he limped around, cleaned his secret abode, packing up all his gear. Today was the day he was to move out of his rented little hideaway, notifying the Publican, who was a little disappointed, knowing of Rob's departure. He had become quite attached to Rob over the last couple of weeks and looked upon him as the son he'd never had, having enjoyed him helping with a few of the heavier jobs around the pub. Rob handed over the keys, shook his hand, and thanked him for his help.

Rob preferred to stash his suitcase of clothes, Kaitlin's books, and a few other small articles in a large locker at the local railway station for the time being. On completion of this task, he returned to his secret hideaway for the last time. Mainly for sentimental reasons, Rob had to visit it one more time. His leg now playing havoc, and the pain heightening from him walking around so much on it. He then sadly left the secret hideaway, Riding his motorbike back to the biker property as the funeral of his so-called biker mates was being held today. The story associated with the incident had been built into an incredibly wild tale for the press to administer, establishing the Police Officer as a real hero. If only he knew Rob had witnessed the whole scene.

Only a small crowd gathered at the funeral. Carlos and Rolf, were cremated. Rob had secretly supplied the money to the vicar, having him do most of the organizing as he didn't really have much idea when dealing with the dead, preferring not to be involved in this situation anyway.

When the funeral was over, he had Emily drop him back in the town of his little hideaway without giving away any details, explaining that he would go to the local Doctor in this town, as nobody would know him and get his leg seen to. The story was almost working on her, although it didn't feel right. Besides, she was concerned about his leg and wondered who had seen to it the previous night. This time Emily chose to investigate the situation further herself, being incredibly cautious. From a distance, observing Rob getting into a hired car and driving off down the road, she followed cautiously in hot pursuit. Although staying quite a distance behind other vehicles, she still maintained sight of his whereabouts.

Totally mortified as he actually drove up to Fred's farm, Emily pulled over off of the road to remain inconspicuous. He drove up to Fred's farmhouse and actually ventured inside. Man, what was he up to? She was genuinely amazed by his antics, although with no definite facts to go by. Emily smiled to herself at his intelligence, wondering how long this little escapade had been going on and how he had actually come to meet Kaitlin, recalling now, times in conversation when unnoticeable he probed her for information about Kaitlin. Emily was still unsure but trusted that he had found happiness and now realized as much as he had tried to conceal his joy. It had been quite noticeable but only to herself, and Brian although it hadn't been until now that she had pieced together the pieces, and she still had so much more to find out.

It was time to head back to the biker property. Brian would worry, thinking maybe she was giving birth somewhere, but she loved him dearly and appreciated some of his maternal instincts that had developed over recent times. Approaching fatherhood had definitely brought out the best in him. If anything, he had become so much more responsible. She, too, was glad to have someone to care so much about her. She looked forward to becoming a mother, thinking it beats the hell out of being involved in drugs. Now realizing what a long way she had come, it had been a hard road, but it was worth going through to come out on top. She was proud of herself for turning a bad situation into a constructive one.

Pulling into the local deli to buy some fresh veggies,

there, to her surprise, was Kaitlin, doing a bit of shopping as well. Immediately Kaitlin held out her arms to greet Emily, although it was challenging to cuddle her being so pregnant. Kaitlin told her how healthy she looked and felt her tummy, seeing if she could feel any sign of life. They both laughed. Then she explained to Emily she'd met a guy and showed her a photograph. Emily now had everything confirmed solidly in her mind. She prayed Kaitlin wouldn't get hurt, as she was too nice a person. Kaitlin explained how she had met him, where he lived, and innocently filled her in on some details. One thing for sure, he definitely was shrewd, but he sounded like a different personality than the Rob she knew, and Emily recalled her mother's old saying, "It's the quiet ones you need to watch out for," so appropriate in this case. It's incredible how someone can actually conceal themselves behind silence.

Emily would say nothing of her discovery. It didn't pay to be a big mouth, especially when this could be a blessing in disguise. Maybe there was hope that he could turn out to be a really decent sort of a person.

Emily thought as she drove home, hoping that all would be well in the future. Rob stayed with Kaitlin again that night, feeling so good just to be with her. She really brought out the best in him. They discussed the show in town the following night, neither being able to go and finding excuses to cover their real reasons. He left early in the morning as the sun was rising, kissing Kaitlin tenderly, leaning over her in the romantically adorned warm double bed, explaining that he really loved her genuinely no matter what happened. She felt it was a strange but remarkable statement to make and, thinking nothing more of it, drifted back into a peaceful sleep. Before he left, limping slightly still over to the line to hang out Fred's shirt amongst the washing, hoping no one had missed it, he retrieved the knapsack of money and jacket from under the tank stand. Thank God it was still there. Not the most appropriate place one would generally hide three-quarters of a million dollars, but under the circumstances, it had served well. Rob realized he left some things on the antique writers' desk stand in the large entrance hallway. He limped in then suddenly tripped over something that didn't seem to be there initially. He stood up swiftly, ready for flight and fight. Kaitlin wandered sleepily down the hallway to see what had happened.

"Oh my god, it's Jimmy. Jimmy moved, then hovered behind Kaitlin. Rob froze, demanding. "Who's Jimmy?". Kaitlin quick to respond, "It's Freds deceased Father. Hes a ghost here in this house apparently." Jimmy waved his finger at Rob in a threatening way. Rob became angry for a second. "You look like you've seen a ghost," Kaitlin said. "I saw him, I saw Jimmy, this is the second time I have seen this ghost," said Rob coldly. Jimmy grows bigger behind Kaitlin, growling silently at Rob. "Don t worry, he's a friendly ghost. It's Fred's' dad, a warm, lovable larrikin of a character. Rob stared Jimmy down. Kaitlin turned to look, but Jimmy had disappeared. She smiled happily. "He protects us all here in Fred's farmhouse. Rob stated, "I am sure Jimmy does." Feeling suddenly under threat and not knowing what the hell to believe, or if Kaitlin was maybe even teasing him. Thinking to himself surely this could not be real.

Confused, Rob drove back to store his money in the locker at the local railway station, along with the rest of his gear.

Returning his hire car, he paid his bill then hitchhiked back to the biker property, being lucky enough to score a lift all the way with a trucky, who was passing through on his run to Queensland. Boy, what a talker, thought Rob. He would have made a great coach driver on a deluxe by keeping travellers on the bus continually amazed. Maybe he, too, had missed his true calling in life.

On arriving back on the biker property, Rob placed his badly damaged motorbike in the large biker shed. Today he would pull some of it apart and do some work on it. He opened the massive shed door. The perfume was so strong. No wonder that dope had smelt slightly strange. He opened all the windows of the shed, airing the place. It grew dark. The small group of the bikers had dinner, Emily cleaning up while they all were excited to be going out celebrating dressed in the best clothes they had.

Rob still limping helped Emily with the dishes and found the opportunity appropriate as no one else was around. He stopped her from her domestic chores, looking her straight in the eye, saying, "Emily, between you and me, if anything hap-pens to me, under the floorboards in the corner of my room is some money. Not much, but it may come in handy for you, Brian, and the baby." She was really caught off guard, wonder-ing what he was up to next. She thanked him, continuing her chores in silence. Emily dismissed the discussion. Everybody drove off the biker property. Rob was left alone, working in the big biker shed. He'd set up the oxy welder with some of the guys before they'd left for the Saturday nights Shindig Show in the local town. Peace at last. He looked at his bike. It needed a great deal of work done on it since its involvement in the accident. He touched it and stared admiringly at it, then walked back up to the biker house to organize a few minor details.

Sixteen

Fred, Jo, Wally, and Kaitlin drove Wally's truck up to the grape pickers' shed across the way from the biker property, all dressed in black, jumping out into the darkness, armed with torches, tools, and ab sailing equipment, well armed for their approaching transgression. All were nervous but excited by their incredible plot to recover the magical love potion. Observing the area cautiously, ensuring the place was void of human life, Fred sneaking around stealthily like a pro, to his astonishment, he found that the door of the biker shed was actually unlatched. Standing back then with great scepticism, he entered seamlessly without disturbing the slightest object, attest in his mind that there was, without doubt, not one definite sign of life.

Fred questioning everything for a moment. Things felt too easy. He was almost disappointed. He never had a chance to utilize the break-and-enter techniques he had been practicing so religiously over the last couple of days. Now was not the time to dwell on the present state of the affair. The timing was crucial. He quietly signalled to the other three for assistance. They carefully loaded themselves up with the magical love perfume boxes, packing them with accelerated veracity into Wally's truck. Replacing them with boxes almost identical containing similar bottles full of methylated spirits and inflammable oil.

Working quickly and quietly, Fred's adrenaline was pumping, realizing the oxygen bottle close by and seeing the disheveled motorbike, glancing to admire it himself. He'd never had a motorbike but had a passion for them. Fred worked rapidly to set up his equipment for the would-be best performance he would remember secretly and hopefully, happily for the rest of his life. Hoping after the three had invested so much money in buying the equipment that it would work. Should a failure occur, they would be up shit creek. His only wish at the moment is that someone in the future could make a video of the oncoming saga, but the technology wasn't around yet to do that. Fred was glad these bastards would pay for stealing the girls' work in the first place, and deep down to some degree, he had resented Emily's disloyalty even if it had been so purely innocent.

The night air was freezing. All were organized and now sitting back patiently, watching the house, waiting in anticipation for their prey to arrive home. No doubt this would certainly blow their minds and be far more exaggerated and dramatic, as Fred expected that no doubt they would be pissed and stoned, and he hoped that this incident wouldn't bring on the birth of Emily's child. Even though Fred sought revenge, it wasn't to that extreme, and he sure as hell didn't want to feel guilty living with that fact. Anyway, it was Kaitlin's and Jo's idea to blow the shed up after the rest of the effects had taken place. They whispered quietly among themselves, growing impatient. It was now 2:00 am. The show was supposed to finish at 1:00 am. The waiting was the worst part of this saga.

The small van pulled up. Emily and her boyfriend climbed out. They appeared to be cold sober, but Fred had already surmised that they would be. Then up behind them, hanging out of the beat-up old station wagon, was a couple of yahoo bikers, if ever he had seen. So pissed was one of the bikers, he fell out of the car, had to crawl, then he just spewed everywhere. How revolting. It reminded Fred of his school days when they would have camping weekends away. Thank God he grew out of that habit fast. Man, he could see why. The crouching four took up their positions. One of the bikers turned, facing them, to do a leak. Wally's face grimaced in the dark as Kaitlin regarded Wally. She thought Wally might be tempted to play a trick on the biker, and she frowned at Wally.

On that note, Fred gave the signal, and off went a thunder-some bang in the biker shed. When the fireworks exploded. Out from the rubber hose came a large amount of white smoke, making a wide screen in front of the biker shed, disguising the four, which would also assist them in their getaway truck being well camouflaged and the sound of it starting up not detected.

The bikers ran screaming, the explosion scaring the hell out of them. The perfume bottles heated up dramatically from the rising temperature in the biker shed and were beginning to ignite and explode. Next minute the oxygen blew up, flames leaping recklessly about the interior of the biker shed. The place was ablaze with high thick raging flames of fire. Terrified Emily ran in to ring on the landline, alert the fire brigade, and seek Rob's help. Jo, Fred, Wally, and Kaitlin jumped speedily into the truck, taking off down the track completely unnoticed, drowned out by all the commotion, Wally and Fred were ecstatic by the completion of a well-executed heist, and they thought it a very professional mission accomplished.

The fire spread thick and fast, engulfing everything in its path, even destroying some of the grapevines in the vicinity. Emily fetched the garden hoses to protect the biker house from going up in massive engulfing flames. The other couple of bikers were of no help to Emily and Brian and totally useless in their present drunken, stoned state. The country CFS Fire Brigade eventually arriving, parts of Rob's motorbike explosively blew straight through the roof of the large biker shed, exploding on impact. The expensive Custom Car caught on fire, and the petrol within ignited like a bomb adding even more explosives to the fire. The small nearby back shed exploded as it contained volatile inflammable chemicals, which the bikers had used for growing their dope crops. Brian fought for quite some hours with the CFS to put out the fire. Emily was indeed proud of him. She searched the Biker house and property, looking for Rob, but he too was nowhere to be found. Emily wondered what course of action he had actually played, if any, in this sudden misfortune, remembering back to his words in the kitchen that night. All trace of the tubing and equipment used by Fred was totally destroyed in the fire, therefore pointing no evidence of arson nor to them retrieving any of the magical love potions.

The local Police Officer and a Fire Expert from the City

were called in straight away to investigate the forensic side. Still, they could not come up with any other reason than the oxygen welder having caused an excessive amount of heat which ignited everything in the shed. Therefore, the contents of the bottles in the boxes, being so highly inflammable anyway, had ignited, causing the explosion, friction, and heat and also exploding the oxygen cylinder. The motorbike, naturally being filled with petrol, added to the massive explosion. Unfortunately, there was a half-burnt skeleton, and fragments of burnt clothing lay on it. They were Rob's clothes. The detectives went back into the house to talk to Emily, who identified them as being the clothes Rob had been wearing that night. She was in total shock, not realizing till that particular moment that Rob had been killed. Emily collapsed from shock as Brian quickly caught her. Lowering her to the ground gently. Soothing her emotionally. Brian himself was dumbfounded and speechless.

The Police Officer explained it would have happened so quickly there would have been no way he could have gotten out of there alive anyway. Emily cried while Brian comforted her. She was really nervous and shaking. The Police Officer suggested she lay down and rest. It was the early morning hours, and fighting the fire most of the night had taken a toll on everybody. Exhausted and restless, Emily cried herself to sleep. She also worried about how it would affect Kaitlin now. Emily would have to tell her tomorrow. She must go and see Kaitlin. Emily had to right the wrong. She had to grow up and take some form of responsibility and be honest.

When Emily rose, most of the other remaining bikers, heavily hungover, had collected their gear together and were about to get the hell out of the biker property feeling it was part of a set up by the Mafia or Police Officers. Emily and Brian decided to stay and wait to clean the place up as they really had nowhere to go yet. They were in some ways quite settled here, with her unable to travel at this stage. Unsure of what to do regarding Rob's death, she, in her own mind, suddenly recalled him telling her he was an orphan, although she was sure he belonged to an incredibly wealthy famous family in Sydney. Confused in her present state of mind, she opted for a short remembrance service. There couldn't be much of a funeral as, basically, his body had already been almost cremated. She got herself together and went to see the Priest, who organized a remembrance service for Rob. Emily didn't even know his last name and felt that at least she would be able to pay her last respects and now having to muster enough strength to explain the story to Kaitlin, but would she believe her? This was the question. Kaitlin seemed and appeared from a distance to be so in love with him as Rob was with her. How on earth was she going to handle this. How could she face Fred, Jo, and Kaitlin regarding the magical love potion theft and many other issues? Brain and Emily started cleaning up the place once the forensic fireman completed his investigation. The local Police Officer, who seemed unusually quite happy about the whole fire incident, paid them a visit for the last time regarding the case. Instructing them the case was closed.

Seventeen

It was Sunday. Kaitlin thought being such a beautiful sunny day, she would drive to Rob's little cottage and surprise him with a picnic lunch. She really felt she had something to celebrate, and now she would tell him all about them rescuing their magical love potion. Kaitlin thought she could trust him, aflutter that there was so much to say to him. She arrived at the little cottage, knocking on the door, his car nowhere to be seen. Maybe she would sit in the warm sunshine and wait on his verandah. The door opened, her face surprised by the appearance of a huge Fraulein woman holding a mop in one hand and a broom in the other.

Kaitlin was so shocked and so devastated on finding that he had vacated the premises, feeling such a great disappointment What an empty heartbreaking void. She felt betrayed and desolate. He'd left without even saying goodbye. She drove home slowly, tears of bitter heartbreak sliding down her cheeks. On pulling up in the driveway at Fred's Farmhouse, she found Emily's van parked there, to Kaitlin's surprise. The four of them sat at the table while Emily spilled her guts about everything. Wally felt uncomfortable with all the seriousness of it all. He left the room, wandering outside to attend to Fred's garden. Knowing this would be a double blow for Kaitlin as Dave's death had nearly destroyed her. Kaitlin and Emily sobbing in between conversations. Although not divulging any information to Emily that they may have done anything to cause the explosion, Kaitlin secretly felt it was partly her fault. After all, it was her suggestion to blow up the biker shed to remove all the evidence. Emily left in a veil of gloom and darkness after she completed her story.

The four then discussed the terrible ordeal and felt so bad that someone had actually lost their life over what seemed now to be a ridiculous magical love potion. For such a gimmick of an idea, it certainly had taken its toll and caused so many emotional roller coaster situations. They questioned its worth and wondered if they had even done the right thing moving to the country in the first place. Kaitlin was totally morbid, having now lost the two loves of her life. Feeling her world was torn apart and unsure as to her direction in life and what was she to believe, in regards to Rob, she couldn't quite understand these stories, refusing to believe it was the same guy, the gentle caring man she had come to know and feel so deeply for. The funny thing was said Kaitlin to Wally and Jo, "my intuition is telling me it can't be right." Wally responded with his reassuring words of wisdom. I've always told you to follow your intuition, as it never fails you." Jo and Fred nodded, agreeing in silence. Concerned she may be in denial and perhaps crash emotionally later at which time they would be there for her.

The following day slowly came, and Emily collected

Kaitlin, driving to the remembrance service together, a sad, miserable, but very small scene.

Emily called in for coffee when they returned back to Fred's farmhouse. About to depart for the biker property, Emily discovered she had a flat tire. At this stage, she became incredibly uptight and had the feeling she couldn't take anymore, almost losing control of her temper. Bending down abusing the tire, her water broke, causing her to have severe contractions. Kaitlin hurried her inside. Jo rang an ambulance, but the local ambulance arrived just in time to witness Kaitlin assisting in delivering the little baby boy, who Emily instantly named Rob. Brian came, and she departed for the Hospital in the ambulance with Brian in tow. Amongst all the sadness and commotion, a new life was born, and it really was a wonderfully joyful experience, relieving the present morbid situation.

Wally returned to Adelaide. Then Jo, Fred, and Kaitlin decided that they would return to the city to market their product after hanging around for a week. Their project, when put on the market, did incredibly well after only a few short days. They left most of the organizing to Wally, who also received a generous cut of the money. While back in the city with such excellent results, the three then had to return to the country to tie up their loose ends and pack up all their things.

The three had almost become an overnight success, now having ample money to pursue their dreams. Although Kaitlin still remained broken hearted, she had plenty to keep her mind presently occupied. Kaitlin went to the biker property where Emily and Brian were still living, even though it was partly burnt down and had not been repaired since the fire. In conversation, Kaitlin told them about the lovely cozy cottage Rob had rented out down the road and suggested they look at renting that out from the Publican, especially now they had a little one. It seemed much more appropriate and more homely for a small family. The threesome not telling Emily about all the money they had now accumulated from selling their magical love potion. They left all the furniture to Emily and her boyfriend. Emily invited them to their small but happy wedding, which was held on Saturday. Before Emily left the property, she suddenly remembered Rob's words regarding the money stored under the floorboards, thinking that it would only be such a small amount anyway. To her surprise, it came to $50,000, which then allowed them to actually buy the cottage.

Emily and Brian came through the whole situation rather well off and a lot better within themselves for the experience. Emily's now-husband took up a job with the local council and decided to put himself through night school so he could really make something of his life. Emily overwhelmed with happiness, now had everything she could ever want. Inner happiness and contentment.

Jo and Fred decided to go into town to do their last grocery shop for their last couple of days. While driving from the supermarket car park, Police Patrol cars emerged from everywhere. There was an onslaught of Police parked surrounding the local Police Station. The city Police attacked in military operation and were handcuffing the local Police Officers and arresting the bad guys as other Police Officers looked on in disbelief.

Fred, Jo, and Kaitlin looked on with shock and were so happy they were all being arrested for their crimes. What exactly they were being arrested for, the three did not know and as Kaitlin looked on, spoke gently "Karma" Jo and Fred silently nodding to agree wholeheartedly.

On their return, they all decided then and there to pursue their dreams as life was so short. Jo and Fred were taking off to settle in Melbourne for a little while, to grow the magical love potion business. Wally and Kaitlin worked together for a week back in Adelaide, establishing the company, bringing home some credited awards. However, without Kaitlin knowing it, someone was spying on her, aware of her every move and constantly following her. All of a sudden, feeling very depressed, she then decided to return to go and stay at her family's beach house. While shopping, Kaitlin saw an ad for a trip to the Incas in Peru. Kaitlin had thought this might be a good idea. She felt she owed herself a holiday. She booked a trip on an 11-day trek. This would take her through the mountains of the lost civilization of the Incas. Within days Kaitlin had left for the destination. It was such a rushed trip.

She trekked for four arduous days up a hundred-kilometer mountain in Peru with an interpreter, guide, and a small team. It was fascinating and worlds away from anything she had known. It was such a historical event for Kaitlin, filled with incredible restorative energy from the surrounding unusual vegetation and prolific landscape.

Standing finally at the top of Machu Pichu, just as she had seen in her dream and visualization many times. Overlooking the lost civilization, the views breathtaking, overwhelmed by her feelings-if only Rob could be with her, she missed Dave so, so terribly too. Deep in thought and in the moment her eyes teared up with sadness at her devastatingly losses as she forlornly stared out onto the extraordinary landscape, tears quietly rolling down her beautiful cheeks. A gentle hand tapped her on the shoulder, leaving her momentarily flabbergasted. It was, to her total astonishment, Rob. He grabbed her and held her so lovingly. She was so stunned she could not speak. Rob proceeds to tell his side to the story, explaining he had only faked the death to get away from the drug scene with all the money, also explaining that he had been following her closely for the last two weeks. She filled him in on the details about Emily and Brian, and the child, about the magical love potion perfume, and all the other information that now fit together to shed light and make the picture very clear.

Rob explained to Kaitlin, that he was from a very famous wealthy family in New South Wales. He had tried to cut himself off from them when he was younger. In his rebellion, Rob joined the Police Force without his family knowing, then became a detective. He went undercover in this instance to blow the drug ring apart, using the bikie group as a cover-up to catch the corrupt Police Officers and their Mafia counterparts, who were also involved. But now, Rob must return home to resolve the family feud. He also asked Kaitlin if she would forgive him for what he had done. If there was any chance of that and if she was willing, he wanted her to go with him. She was the only women he had ever wanted in his life. He was fully committed, if she would forgive him.

Kaitlin was very overwhelmed and had to sit down and digest all the information Rob had just shared with her. Kaitlin took a deep breath. They sat in silence together on the cliff, he slipped his arm around her shoulder very lovingly, not speaking for another moment. She actually felt that he was telling the truth. Kaitlin briskly instantly stood up. Rob didn't know what she was going to say. She turned to him, reached out happily with her hand, and said," Come on, then we best go." Rob smiled so happily with a weight lifted off his heart. They walked down from the mountain into a bright new future with plenty of happiness and money to show for it, and now Kaitlin had ample travel material to write about. Rob's part in the biker group and involvement with the Mafia would never be uncovered by the Police. So many facts had been covered up. Many real criminals were involved with the drug ring, who were now in jail, or in hiding and nowhere to be found. No one would want to start digging up facts about any discrepancies about whether some of those people even existed. Too many people had buried all traces of any crimes they had committed in this case. The local country Police Officers involved in the drug racket had been charged and sent to prison.

Kaitlin and Rob left the Inca Trek and the mountains of Peru, happy, contented, in love and free to get on with their lives, and that would be a whole other story given "KAJO," the magical love potion and its powerful success.

The End

About the author

Karen Power has a unique and fresh approach to storytelling. Her writing draws on the essence of her life experiences and inherent natural affinity with the metaphysical.

She has worked as a nurse, screenplay writer, background extra, and has written several novels and screenplays. Karen is the producer, writer and director of a short film titled "Raphael", showcasing on Prime Video Amazon, which has won several International Awards.

Karen is the author of *The Lighthouse,* a supernatural romance thriller; *The Golden Phoenix,* a supernatural crime romance thriller; and *KAJO,* an Australian adventure romance. Her work is available in paperback, e-book and audiobook formats from your favourite bookstores. You can order online, or enquire with your local bookshop or library.

For more information about Karen's current and future works, please visit: **www.karenpowerfilms.com.au**

Thank you for supporting an Australian writer of original, creative content. If you have enjoyed this book, please consider writing an online review.

www.ingramcontent.com/pod-product-compliance
Lightning Source LLC
Chambersburg PA
CBHW070401200726
48294CB00003B/1025